THE INVISIBLE HAND

DOUGLAS COLE

Sea Crow Press

ALSO BY DOUGLAS COLE

Drifter

The Cabin at the End of the World

The White Field

The Blue Island

The Gold Tooth in the Crooked Smile of God

Bali Poems

The Dice Throwers

Western Dream

Interstate

The Ghost

PRAISE FOR DOUGLAS COLE

In this mesmerizing book, Mr. Cole combines the lyrical and poetic ease of the writer with the gripping rhythm of musical fours. Told in four sections, each part twirls and dances with characters circling back on themselves, repeating the refrain of the ever-present, ever-changing invisible hand, a metaphor connecting each striking vignette. As with his novel, *The White Field*, in *The Invisible Hand*, Cole continues his keen ability to drop you into a story from the first sentence and not let you go.

—SHERYL J. BIZE-BOUTTE, AUTHOR OF
*BETRAYAL ON THE BAYOU, BACK TO THE
BAYOU: THE TASSIN VALLEY SAGA
CONTINUES* AND OTHER WORKS

Douglas Cole writes with real American grit. His novel *The Invisible Hand* shares a sequence of seemingly disparate stories that come together in subtleties and hard moments of brutal clarity that toy with your emotions … all of them. This novel has at times a noirish feel, and at others a reaching, yearning humanism. You will feel for the characters, worry about them, flinch at their vulnerability, but never want to look away. Cole has woven a web that's full of spiders, and you, the fly, will never feel so happy to be devoured."

—ACE BOGGESS, AUTHOR OF *THE PRISONERS*
AND *A SONG WITHOUT A MELODY*, AND
EDITOR AT EVENING STREET PRESS REVIEW

Things "happen and there is no other way that they could have happened, ever. If that's fate..., I guess I believe in fate," confesses Jack, one of the characters haunted by difficult circumstances in Douglas Cole's, *The Invisible Hand*. As darkly glittering as a country night sky or the alleyway puddles that reflect a big city's glistening high-rises, *The Invisible Hand* explores the lives of those struggling on the fringes. Prepare to be gripped by Cole's weaving, lyrical language and the absolutely strange: "Sometimes, the noise comes from his skin or from under the skin." While each of his characters struggles with loss, aimlessness and a sense being invisible, Cole remains in control, the invisible hand guiding us through these characters' worlds, no matter how shadowy and warped they appear.

—**CASSANDRA LANE**, EDITOR IN CHIEF OF *L.A. PARENT MAGAZINE* AND AUTHOR OF *WE ARE BRIDGES*, A LYRICAL MEMOIR RECONSTRUCTING THE LOST HISTORY OF A BLACK AMERICAN FAMILY AND ONE OF THE BEST BOOKS OF 2021 PICKED BY NPR.

ACKNOWLEDGMENTS

Portions of this work have appeared in the following journals: *Adelaide, Chautauqua, Concho River Review, Crucible, Impspired, Knot Magazine, Lotus-Eater Literary Magazine, Louisiana Literature, Page and Spine, Shooter Magazine, Solstice Lit (Nominated for The Pushcart and Best of the Net), and Typehouse.*

I would like to thank Anastasia Drost for helping see the vision and Janet Steen for her ever-precise refinements and Mary Petiet for bringing this book into the world.

For Jenn

THE INVISIBLE HAND

PART ONE

A RANDOM WALK

She watched the jury come in. And with a dream detachment that sometimes hits people in life-changing moments whether they know it or not, she watched them take their seats and turn to face the man accused, all wearing the same emotionless expression, all waiting as the judge summoned the verdict. The Bailiff floated ghost slow and transferred the verdict note. The judge took the paper and opened it so slowly it made an audible rasp. That's all it was, too, nothing but a slip of paper with one or two words written on it, probably in pencil, spelling out the fate of the man before her.

And she watched this man, her father, as he half rose and was half lifted by a guard from his chair. He stood there, hands at his sides and attached to a chain encircling his waist, wearing the orange coveralls of the convict already. And the fire door appeared behind him hot white at the center and blue at the edges, elusive to direct gaze and partly designed by her testimony. When the judge spoke, his mouth moved in slow motion, his voice a monotone, and the only thing in his string of phrases she heard was the word–Guilty. Her father turned then as though he too had been rehearsed, his face showing no expression. This was indeed a rehearsed moment. Hadn't he said more than once to never show your emotions? That it gives people power over you? So, she wondered as he moved forward in his hobbled gait and turned just enough to allow his eye to meet hers in a moment during which if anything she may have detected a smile, what did her own face reveal?

Riding home on the bus she was aware of time speeding up. Moments, even the brief span of time from leaving the courthouse to getting on the bus, were shooting by her and through her in complicated symphonies of individual faces and wind and changes in the horsetail clouds, conversations, radio voices and music coming from the cars, whirring drones and laughter, stirring up, speeding up to a high-pitched whine. And there was no getting them back and no way of knowing just what had been lost.

The bus was a chamber of iron heat, stench of city sewer and smoke and foul people odor. No amount of shrinking kept her free of contact. One man lay reeking and stretched out on an entire seat. A few gray outlines of shadow-keepers and other hungers hovered nearby too, but she knew by now how to adjust to them when they were on the scene. The bus bounced through the city and the dust plumed behind it. The sun was low, orange and veiled in heat waves, burning over low hills and black-etched cutouts of homes and through palm trees that glowed like fabulous aliens. People got off as she rode on, and she watched passively as the homes shrank and the yards filled up with old vehicles and roads became more lunar. Then the sleeping man rose, his face a quick-shifting mask of anger and bewilderment, his hair like grease-clumped feathers. She stared strategically ahead past his scan-glances as the bus came to her stop. She felt him watching her as she descended to the street. He was the only passenger left, looking down at her through the window as the bus pulled away.

She walked the short distance to her home as a truck swept by sending up a rooster tail of dirt. Her head was a hive of bees. More houses were abandoned now. Squatters had drifted in, but where did the other people go? Where could they go? The road in front of their houses was once the main road but now ran parallel to the city, a grimy ring around the daylight business district with dollar motels and boarding houses, gloomy spaces dying but never dying off. Yet it was still a heavily used thoroughfare because it had no stop lights or stop signs, from the wastelands to the cooling centers, and people who knew used it to avoid escaping crowds on the main road and because the police never patrolled it. She passed dirt yards where dogs slept on porches in front of screen doors behind which televisions glowed in rooms full of phantom auroras. She passed but did not make eye contact with the man watering his patio who stood shirtless and bloat-bellied with a cigar stub ground into his countenance. Then she passed through the little chain link gate and up to the porch of her own home, unlocked the door and went in.

Inside the house the air was hot and still and silent. They owned very little and little was left. Her father pawned whatever he could to pay the lawyer who was expensive but in the end little better than the court-appointed one who eventually took over. There were no photographs, no mementos of any kind, nothing certainly of her mother. They owned the house, but now the state would confiscate it, as they do in cases like this. The lightning flash-crackle of an opening appeared on her left but was elusive and vanished when she turned her head. She could still smell her father's smoke and alcohol and aftershave, and it nearly made her pass out.

She went to her room and sat on the edge of the bed for a long time. She sat there as the light faded, sat there unmoving, and in brief spasms of self-consciousness realized that she was thinking nothing at all. The light drained out of the room, and she sat there in darkness, not so much because she was depressed but because she didn't know what to do. There was no one to tell her where to go, and so she sat. She was not particularly hungry. Then a thought came to her, like someone spoke into her head. And she stood and looked around her room and saw her backpack, and with a little grin she could never have explained to anyone, she packed a few clothes, a coverless book of Russian poetry, a notebook and the family gun her father said she'd need and would use at some point because it was a part of their lives so long that to lose it was to let a fire die and might offend ancestors causing them to stir and become involved again against their wishes. She put the pack on and went into the kitchen where she confronted the array of her father's liquor bottles and took them into the living room and poured the contents on the bare wood floor and lit a match and dropped it in the pool of liquid and watched as a lovely blue flame whipped up like electric hair and rose in a glorious fire.

She walked out the door and left it wide open behind her and did not look back. In the windows of houses and windshields of cars along the street she saw the glowing, shaking little fins of fire waving goodbye as she walked away.

When she boarded the Greyhound bus, yet another bus in an uncountable line of buses she had boarded in her lifetime, only a handful of people were evenly dispersed throughout the seats, so she was able to take a row of her own. She put her backpack onto the overhead rack and sat down and waited. They were a silent collection on that bus. The cabin lights lit the windows into dark mirrors so that she could barely see outside except for the people bent at the counter in the terminal café that was well-lit from within. Her own face and the faces of the rest of the passengers were framed and still and trapped in the darkness that roared outside. Then the driver boarded the bus and punched on the engine and rolled the destination sign through a succession of names until it stopped on the words San Diego. Another man outside slammed down the cargo covers. The driver pulled the doors shut, and they were almost ready to pull out of the station when a man came running across the parking lot shouting at the driver, Stop!

The bus was just beginning to roll. The driver grunted once and jerked to a stop and the man outside smiled and lifted a hand as if both thanking the driver and waving to an audience. The driver opened the doors and the man climbed aboard, carrying a small brown travel case of soft, spotted leather. He grinned and said, I thank you, bowing to the driver who only nodded and twisted an upper lip. Then the driver put the bus in gear and pulled forward before the man had a chance to take a seat. The man lurched to one side but caught himself quickly and with a kind of dancer's grace started down the aisle, taking the shifts and changes in motion some-where in the center of his body and moving with his legs a little apart, as easily as an experienced sailor walking the deck of a ship. There were any number of seats he could have chosen and had a row to himself, but he stared straight forward and smiled and threw his satchel up on the rack right beside her backpack and sat in the seat next to her so close his leg rested against hers.

Howdy, he said. I'm Jack. He extended a hand.

She felt herself pulling back inside but shook his hand anyway.

She was thinking to say something like, please take another seat, or, I'd rather be alone, thank you, but instead all she said was, Hi, turning her head quickly in his direction but not looking at his eyes so that all she really saw was the blurred shape of his face and the knife point of a sideburn.

What's your name?

My name…. she hesitated, then said, Sara.

Very nice to meet you, Sara. Whew! I nearly missed this one, didn't I? I don't think the driver likes me though because of that last-minute jump. And he laughed a little and said, But I'm just coming back from Mexico, you know? They do things a little different there. And she felt him staring straight at her so frankly and unflinchingly that she felt the heat of his eyes. Beautiful country, Mexico. Beautiful place, although you have to be careful, for sure, you know, if you're an outsider. It's better if you speak the language. Me gusta la lengua mucho, entonces fue facile por mi. Comprende? You understand any of that? She shook her head. I was on the west coast just South of Mazatlán in a little town called San Blas. Heard of it?

For a moment she wasn't sure why he was speaking to her. How could he not see? His Spanish was awful, that much was clear, and when she realized she had better say something just to keep him at bay or else allow him to burrow in with more questions about why she was so silent or why she was so unfriendly, she said, No, I haven't.

Oh, pristine, untouched. It's just a fishing village. Nothing there to attract your typical tourist. At all. No clubs or donkey shows or jai alai or abandoned missions. Just a few restaurants and a whorehouse, but the beaches have the widest, flattest plane, you know, so the waves break forever. See it? They rise up a mile or so offshore and just fall and keep falling all the way in. It's truly paradise.

Then why did you leave? She didn't want to encourage any of this conversation with him. The words had come of their own accord.

Why, he said, a grin rising. It's a strange story, really. Kind of a mistaken identity thing.

In the fishing village?

He leaned back a little as if to take a more careful look at her. Well listen to you, he said, and here I thought I was going to do all the talking till we reached Balboa Park. Now you're giving me the third degree! Well, I'll tell you, and I can see you're someone I can't lie to. It was me who did the mistaking. I mistook someone, you see? Funny word, huh, mistook? And I'm the kind of person who makes subtle distinctions, you know what I mean? Even if someone is blank as a piece of paper. Like you, for example. Because you see I'm very cautious by nature. Now the man I was looking for was no face in the crowd, no blank slate, right, but I was looking for a stranger with nothing but a verbal description. So where *is* Waldo? I was told to meet this man at a particular place and at a particular time and that he would be expecting me. Maybe with a plan like that I let my guard down a bit. Maybe. So I went to this appointed place at the appointed time, outside the village on a private road with macaws cackling at me like they were warning me about something. A private residence, so not the kind of place you'd expect much confusion about. And what I mean by that is it would be highly unlikely for anyone not supposed to be there to be there. Except for the case of a double-cross, right? I thought about that after. But there were no trackers on me. I've got the sense. You *know* those shadows. So I'm at this appointed place, and it's coming on evening with the sun gone. But light enough, you know, to see enough but not all. And when I approach the house I see the front door's open, which I think odd, like walking into a memory you forgot or something, dreamy weird. I keep going, but just before I go through the door a man comes out, and he's got a gun in his hand! About this I do not lie, and he looks like he's been roughed up a little himself, blood coming from his mouth, and he points that gun at me, so I just stop. I don't say anything. I don't think he saw me clearly yet, you know how when you come out of a dark room. His eyes had the confusion, but it could have been other things at work. I just stand there and look at him. And he says, Mas despacio. And I say, Como? And he says, Mas despacio. And he waves his gun I think for me to come closer, but I do nothing. I'm mas despacioing. Then he points that gun at me more business-like, so I move forward. He sits down on the steps, slow like it hurts to move, and I can see blood, a lot of blood, spreading out on his side and I think maybe he is going to die soon there right in front of me. That hit me as certain. That I thought I knew for sure, and I looked at him, and I watched as he breathed very slowly, like he had to think about every breath to make it happen. And he would close his eyes for a long time and then open them again. I think he was remembering to be there. And then he just leaned down like he was trying to listen to the ground, and as he did that I saw through the doorway that another man was standing back in the shadows of the living room. I tell you, that's when my heart started racing. I got up mas despacio and turned and walked back down the road the way I came. And I'm looking for the guy who told me to go there. He's long gone of course. And I think maybe it's a trick. But I couldn't be sure. But since I'd gone there, since I *was* there, you know, and wherever you go you leave your mark–everything changed, see? The whole case was altered. So now what was I going to do? I was left holding two bags, so to speak, and nobody there was a friend of mine, tell you what. I left immediately. I left that very night. And what happened there, the truth of it and those people and the eventual outcome will always remain a mystery to me, but one that only makes me more glad than I've ever been to be alive and sitting here next to you. You see how that works? Because it's all blurring as it forms, you know? Like a tornado behind me—and then here you are. The perfect ending to the story. Who could have made up such a thing?

Why were you there in the first place? she asked.

He smiled. If I told you I'd have to kill you!

He stopped talking and looked at her. His eyes made her cheeks burn. She turned away but then glanced back at him and that's all it took. He leaned forward slowly, mas despacio, and kissed her, and she let him.

I'm a new character, she thought. I can start from scratch and just invent as I go. And so she began to speak. It was like watching herself outside herself. My mother got real sick, she said. She kept looking out the window through the outline of her own made-up reflection. The land was a flat dry desert of nothing, a world dissolving in distances. Dust devils swirled up along the side of the road, and a dust tail twisted behind the bus like something stampeding after them in the shape of a cloud. She got the flu at first and then she couldn't stand up anymore, said she was too dizzy. We had family over because it was a holiday, and they knew she was sick, but when she started vomiting and couldn't stand for falling, they just left. It was Christmastime, and they were her people, but when she got worse they just left. Father was not there. He was mostly not there. If he was, he'd have told her to stop whining, that it couldn't be that bad. But he'd only say that because he was drunk. I was watching TV. She called from her bed, made me come to her. Her room smelled like sickness. And she said to me, she said, You go and get my diary out of my dresser. I said I don't know where, and she told me which drawer it was in and I got it. She spoke in a whisper in my ear. She wanted to make sure no one else, especially my father, could hear what she was saying. And she said, You take that to the living room—don't read it, now—and you put it on the fire, you understand? I didn't want to do it, and I told her I didn't want to do it. I told her it wasn't necessary and she was going to be just fine and then she wouldn't want me to burn it. I wasn't afraid for myself. I was afraid for her. I mean, I was a little afraid for myself because I didn't want to be alone. But she couldn't help anyway. She was afraid of him, too. But I wanted her to be all right because I loved her and I knew that if I did what she told me it would be giving her more reason not to fight to stay alive. I think she might have wanted to die. She was losing, it looked like. I didn't know everything that was really wrong. I was twelve and I knew but I couldn't tell it. But I knew I wasn't going to burn her diary. I took it though, but I didn't burn it. I thought maybe if I didn't actually burn it she would somehow know, even if she believed I'd burned it. I mean that her spirit would know and in some way that would give her spirit reason to fight. I didn't want to be alone without her. She was never like that before. I was afraid, too, that if I didn't do what she asked me to I might be setting something bad in motion. Something worse. I made her cans of soup and put them by the bed, but she never ate them and they went cold and I poured them out. I slept next to her and felt her shivering. Sometimes she'd say something and I'd say, What? What is it? But she wasn't talking to me. She was in her dreams. I prayed for her to get better. I prayed non-stop. I said God could have some of my time, to just give her some of my time, please. But she didn't get better. She got smaller, and one morning she wouldn't wake up, but she wasn't dead. That's when I called the ambulance and they took her to the hospital. She was far away.

He looked at her, his face close and his expression tight, an odd expression she couldn't read. But she didn't entirely trust faces. She did die, though, in the hospital. And then I burned her diary. I didn't want him to find it because I think he's the reason she wanted me to burn it. She didn't want him to read it, so I burned it, but I suppose that was wrong. I mean, I think now that I should have read it. There might have been something in there that would have saved me time. Changed things.

Well here and I thought I was going to do all the talking, he said. That's quite a story.

Then she looked at him and said, I guess now I have to kill you.

Land. Land and hours passed. Darkness in which not even their faces were visible, their hands interlaced, their mouths close as they talked through the blur of the night.

I've had fifty different jobs, he said.

Not fifty.

Maybe. But I've done work most people would never do.

Like what?

I've dug graves.

You haven't.

I have. I worked in a cemetery in Louisiana.

Did you ever see a ghost?

Heard them.

What did they say?

They said, This place is spooky…

She laughed and in her laughter her breath caught and she buried her face in his shoulder.

There were some gravestones that had worn down, he said, so you couldn't read a name on them. Some broke and sank into the earth. If no one came by or tended them, we just used the spot for another. The dead stacked on top of each other. I know that's a morbid thought.

What else have you done?

Janitor in a school. Nightwatchman. I worked for a catering outfit that did big, blow-out barbeques. That was in Texas. Oscar and his wife Olga ran it. That's their real names. He had a brother out of the navy who probably was a pedophile, but he read Shakespeare. The plays, he said. He liked the plays. He and Oscar were later put in prison for stashing weapons and explosives in their warehouse. Right alongside the food, but I never saw any of that. They were survivalists or something. We did barbeques with six-foot grills full of mesquite. We roasted whole pigs in a pit in the ground. We did barbeques in the desert in the middle of summer with wet rags on our heads and fire burning up our arms. Believe it or not that was the hardest job I ever did. We'd be at it twelve, fifteen hours for these parties. Two thousand people or more. Company parties, mostly, mob parties, birthday parties, weddings. Sometimes people on our crew would pass out in the heat. I'd be alone at that grill turning chicken parts as the flames spat up in my face. Hell can't be much hotter than that job. Hotter than smelting. I did that up in Seattle. At least there we had masks. I worked in a retirement home in Arizona. I worked in a cancer ward in San Francisco. Brain tumors. The worst. People of all ages came rolling in like broken machines on a de-assembly line, poor sick people. Wracked on the inside. Old folks, young folks, children, even. It didn't seem to matter. At first it was hard to take. One little girl came in and got chemotherapy and radiation treatments. She was bald as a newborn baby. She was maybe eight. I went to the bathroom and I just cried like a...that was a hard job to do, at first. I would go home every night and drink a six-pack just to lighten up. I was just an office clerk, setting up appointments, meet and greet. The doctors were robots. I guess you'd have to be. They were smart people, but dumb because they thought they were smart, you know what I mean? A few famous people came in, but I didn't know who they were. I don't keep up on that. I couldn't do it after about six months. That was the last real job I ever had.

What do you mean?

I mean, at first, I thought maybe I'd like to do it as a career, you know? Work in a hospital, take care of people. But I couldn't do it. I couldn't take the suffering. I felt ashamed about that for a while, but I saw what it took to do that job, and I couldn't harden myself that way.

There are different ways, she said. And those must have been the magic words because after that he shut up and smiled and slid his hand over her belly and pressed his teeth against her neck.

The bus pulled off the highway into a small town where a few street lights slid by with their lonely cones of illumination. It was like a mockup of a town with test-dummies and twitching shadows behind dim windows in abandoned buildings and nothing beyond, a ghost town in the middle of nowhere with two-by-fours holding up livery stables and saloon facades. The driver pulled up to a cafe called The Skillet and stopped. He didn't even announce the name of the town. It didn't seem like a regular stop. The lights in the bus came on and some people lifted their heads and stretched and squinted into the night. Some slept on. The driver pushed the door open and dropped to the ground and went into the cafe.

You want something to eat? he asked her.

Sure.

They both got up and went down the aisle along with a few of the other passengers. You know travelin's a lot easier when you have someone to talk to, he said and put his arm around her. She let him. Perhaps it was that she hadn't slept, though she didn't feel the need for sleep, or perhaps it was the unreality of the journey, being on the road with no home now behind her drawing her back and nothing really ahead of her drawing her to a destination, but it was all right, being with him like this, feeling like this. Her father was a jail-keeper in jail, now. She never dared to have a friend, let alone a boyfriend. Now, though, she would do this. Now, as an act of defiance, she would do something so simple and so normal. An alarm went off in her head like a fire drill, but she shook her head and glared it away. She let him put his arm around her, and she enjoyed the feeling of the weight of it across her shoulder, even the light way his hand brushed across her collarbone, this new feeling, this new way of being in the world. No wonder she couldn't sleep. Not now that she was finally alive. It was intoxicating.

They slipped into a booth and a waitress floated over like an actress moving in for a closeup.

Anything to drink? she asked as she laid two plastic-coated menus on the table.

You folks serve any beer, here? he asked.

Light or dark?

Light.

I'll have a cup of coffee.

Coffee, girl? You sure you don't want something a little more adventurous? Have a beer with me.

All right. I will.

Light, too? the waitress said.

That's fine.

And why don't you go ahead and bring me some steak and eggs, he said.

I'll just have some toast and jelly.

Toast and jelly? That's not enough food, he said. Eat up. You gotta eat.

Toast and jelly's all I want.

Expressionless and seemingly drained of anything resembling human emotion, the waitress wrote their order down on a green pad and drifted away.

We should be in San Diego by morning, he said. You meeting people?

I have a friend, she said. From school. She moved out there a while ago. We moved south, but last I heard she lives in San Diego. I was hoping to meet up with her.

Are you just visiting or what?

I don't know yet.

That sounds like or what to me. How long were you living in Houston?

About two years. We moved a lot.

Why's that? Your daddy in the military?

She smiled. No. He's not in the military. He changes his name.

Changes his name?

Yeah.

What, he laughed, were you in a witness protection plan? Why'd you move?

Well, I can't say for sure. She drew in a long breath through her nose. She wondered, why all this far away stuff? It was confusing to think about. He had a lot of plans, she said. A lot of irons in the fire, he'd say. That was all he'd say to explain why we had to move.

Then she saw something change in his face. His smile faded for a moment, as if the machinery making the smile stopped responding to command signals, and in its place rose a darker light, some dim and hidden thing, a room of his personality coming to glow. Then he shook his head and smiled again.

Don't that beat the shit out of it, he said.

What?

And here I thought...and he laughed so loud that people in the cafe turned around and looked at him.

What?

Nothing, he said. I just had a different impression of you is all.

What?

I don't know. That you grew up in a proper home. You seem to be...well...it's the way you carry yourself...

I went to good schools, she said. I always went to very good schools.

Catholic?

Yes.

What a world! And you were on the run?

I never said that. We spent most of our time South. I think we were in Mexico for a while when I was little. I remember something about that. He taught me how to shoot a gun, too, said I need to know how to do that.

He was right.

The waitress brought their food. He ate voraciously, looking up at her and shaking his head and smiling, cramming his mouth with food. He drank his beer and she drank hers. She ate her toast and a few bites of his food that he offered to her, feeding her from his own fork. The beer made her head warm, and after she finished it he ordered her another and she drank that too and felt pleasantly confused.

The bus driver pushed himself away from the counter and paid for his meal and went back to the bus. The rest of the passengers followed him. She walked out of the café, and he held his arm around her shoulder tighter now and slapped his stomach and said, Damn, that feels good, then leaned down and kissed her cheek and squeezed her stomach with his other hand and moved it lower and kissed her harder on the neck and said, Honey, I think we may have been made for each other. She pulled back from him as they boarded the bus and took their seats. The doors closed, and the cabin lights went out. The bus moved forward. The passengers turned into cutout versions of themselves. And the town disappeared like it was never really there.

She sat with her head leaned against the window, watching the night invade the road and feeling the rock and jolt of the bus as she drifted beside this man, this other nothing but a shadow in the darkness. She was tired. He had fallen asleep and she was on the verge, though her mind wouldn't release her and seemed to be seeking something and resisted falling away, and for what felt like a lifetime she floated in a warm amniotic brew of phantoms and her own past like blind fish nerving their way through dark sea levels and darting in at her and biting and taking her with them so she saw herself a little girl in the field behind a house they lived in once along the way, and she was alone in the light and the rain soaking the high grass as she waded through wet swales toward a shed at the edge of the light beyond which was a grove of maple trees in full sway from wind that swept along with animating force, so she went up to the shed which was like a weathered outhouse with bare wood grooved and warped and gray with streaks of black descending from the bare nail heads. She opened the door. The smell hit first, damp earth and rot, and the darkness was at first a barrier against which she halted and waited for her eyes to adapt. And slowly appeared the dim outlines of shelves and a narrow dirt floor and a low ceiling beneath which she stooped, cobwebs threaded in the rafters and flumed into thick-silked deep-white mouths along the rotting sill beneath a single window that glowed opaque from years of dust blow and heat and mold-growth. Along the shelves were hundreds of bottles. All of different shapes and sizes and colors. She reached out and touched them, not picking them up at first but simply touching them, and when her hand came away the places where her fingers had made contact glowed. She picked up one bottle and felt the shift of its liquid contents, shook it and heard a splash internally, and with her thumb rubbed the dirt clean from one side so that when she lifted it into the light she could see inside a spiral of ingredients swirling like a tiny tornado. In the top of the bottle was a cork, and she twisted it and pulled it out and the smell hit her like a blow, wretched, putrefied, causing her throat to clench. Her eyes opened. It was like a film swipe then a dissolve, putting her back in the bus again, riding through the boundless night of black imagining the periphery, and with a quick dip back into the borderlands of consciousness she saw the house where she lived with her father and saw it as though she had turned and waited after her last departure, saw it swallowed in a rich and howling fire, becoming a multileveled and rounded furnace with long thin fire strands that opened into eyeless heads wavering for a moment before they popped in the air. Disembodied, extinguished, she rode a watcher through other nights in the back of her father's car, her mother there as they flew through the darkness away from another home, away from a whole series of homes in a series of routine arrivals and departures. Saw herself in house X. She wouldn't unpack but sat with her things inside their boxes, sitting on the bed in a room that was furnished because they always rented furnished homes, sitting among a host of smells, the smells of others, all the lives that tramped through and sat and slept and fretted and dreamed and moved on as she would too. The door of fire wobbled, and she knew there would come a time when it would no longer affect her, would diminish into what she thought was her own life, and that was usually the moment at which her father would call them out to pack again and hurry and go. Gradually she had less and less to pack, leaving bits and pieces behind as they went, books and hairbrushes, chewed-on pencils, photographs and even once her own diary she could not imagine falling into a stranger's hands, feeling acutely exposed though someone much like her would probably end up crawling through that same room and smelling those same alien and oppressive smells and finding her journal and opening it and reading it. She could wander through all those anonymous rooms in succession with her mind in this state, could see herself brooding before television sets as she watched ghosts of the past prance around in reruns, old shows made in a time long before she was born, so familiar from repeated watching she could at times believe they were images from her own life of parallel lives transpiring simultaneously in infinite realms of the possible. Nightmares. Ancient shapes humming like engines with a sound like slurred words intoning derverseran-derverseran-derverseran. A figure draped in robes, hooded, who lifts a cloaked arm at her and silent stands at the foot of the bed and by this presence locks her into place, holds her down without even touching her so that no breath comes, no sound emerges though she tries with all her will to make some sound, tries and would even scream, knowing in some way that the scream would release her but feeling nothing come but a hoarse tight hiss. She opened again back in the bus. She resisted slipping back, but the reach and power of sleep is strong, her body still, her mind fighting the pull of gravity, yet open or closed her eyes still see the contours of the dream, odd floating black spheres that dart and drift and hold and seem to breathe and watch her in the air around her. She thinks if she doesn't look directly at them they'll lose interest and move on. Others are here. Others linger uninvited nearby and would take a peek through her mind if she allowed it, which she does not. She feels her own breath. She feels the mouth of a wolf behind her head. The wolves are circling her, just beyond her vision though she sees them anyway, predatory, stalking peripherally yet somehow unable to get at her, unable to fully locate her. She holds so still they cannot touch her. Instead, she jumps through them, sinks down, then up, away, away, away. Does she fully wake? She doesn't know. It's darker than ever dark. She is somewhere, but she doesn't know where. She must pass through it. She thinks this though she feels unsure how or where she thinks it. She has no body by which to orient her thought, her sense of what she is, that she is at all, and yet she is. That is certain. She is. She knows this, even though all around her is indistinguishable. Extinguished. Blown out. She is. She knows this. She is.

ASYMMETRIC SHOCK

abriel High Bear stood in the line of choir children as the minister went from child to child, asking, Are you a good Christian?

And each child answered, uniformly, in almost the same tone, Yes, I am.

Child to child, the minister went, asking the same question. He asked it with a smile, a proud cant to his back, turning slightly just as each child answered as if to reveal to the congregation the wonder of each face, each soul.

Yes, I am.

When he came to Gabriel, he asked again, in the same tone, with the same slight turn of body, Are you a good Christian?

Gabriel rose in his chest, but he did not say, Yes, I am.

No, he said, I'm a Sagittarius.

And the congregation laughed. Gabriel felt pleased by this and rose even higher in his chest and smiled back at the congregation. The minister smiled, too, but stood his ground and asked the question again.

But are you a good Christian?

This time, Gabriel looked into the eyes of the minister and saw something which would not relent, something that spoke, telling him he had better say the same words the other children said, and he bowed a little, just slightly, and said, Yes, I am. He kept his eyes to the eyes of the minister, and he kept his smile, but he knew in his heart that he was not a good Christian.

After the minister had asked each child the question and received the answers, the children filed past him, and he gave them each a Bible with a red leather cover and a clear plastic box which contained a black string necklace and a black wooden cross. They then took their seats and waited for the sermon to commence. Gabriel held the Bible and the cross in his lap and could not take his eyes off them. The red leather cover was smooth and thick with gold letters on the front that said, Holy Bible. He parted the pages and looked inside and saw a colored drawing of Moses lifting his staff to part the Red Sea. He opened further on and saw Joseph being sold into slavery. He went even further and saw a picture of Jesus standing in a group of children with his arms outstretched. He wanted to put on the cross, but none of the other children had, so he waited. He looked out at the congregation and saw his mother's face. She was smiling at him, but he suppressed a smile of his own.

After the service was over, Gabriel joined his mother and his sister, Branwyn. He showed the cross and the book to his mother. They're just beautiful, she said. But what was that about being a Sagittarius? He shrugged. She wasn't mad, though. In fact, she seemed a little proud and said, You little kidder.

Let me see your pin, he said to his sister. She had been in the older group, and they had each received a gold pin with a little blue cross on it.

No, Branwyn said.

Why not?

She raised her head in that haughty way and said, Because. He knew it was no use asking again.

Do you want to see my cross?

No, she said. I've already got one.

They went into the lounge under the skylight by the fountain and ferns and leaned over the flowerbeds flattening bits of vermiculite between their fingers, waiting while their mother drank coffee and talked. Branwyn moved over by the door and waited. She wouldn't speak to anyone, and Gabriel knew that she looked snobbish but was really shy. Frozen shy. He waited with her, even though she sneered down at him as though she was embarrassed by him. Finally, she said, Go tell Mom it's time to go.

You go tell her.

It's your turn.

No, it isn't.

I went last. It's your turn.

He went over to their mother and took hold of her hand. She continued to talk and he gradually exerted more force on her arm, pulling her away. In just a minute, she said, and she went back to talking. He went and stood by his sister.

You didn't do it right, she said.

You go.

When they got home, Gabriel went down into the basement where his father was working, his shop space framed-in but with no sheetrock or wiring, rows of easels and desks with mounds of sawdust on the floor and sawdust drifting through the air. His father was at the table saw, cutting a board down that would fit into the forms he had designed and patented and was in the process of selling to the university, an order of over two hundred that he had to make himself by the end of the month. Gabriel stood by until the cut was finished, and when his father turned off the saw, he said, Look, I got a wooden cross at church. He held it out on the end of its cord for his father to see. His father pulled back his goggles and looked down at the cross and then picked it up in his dust-covered and calloused hand, squinting at it.

Uh-huh, he said.

I got it for being in choir, Gabriel said.

I know you did. That's nice. I've got to get back to this, so you go on upstairs, now.

Gabriel went up the stairs but stopped and sat down on the landing and watched his father work. His father snapped on the saw and picked up another board from the stack beside him. He slid the board through, precise, clean, the blade loud shrieking Hee-aww-unnnn as it cut the wood, then just the humming of the motor and whir of the naked blade. Gabriel watched, holding his cross in his hand and gauging by mental math on how many of these crosses you could get out of one board. He was not a good Christian, but he wanted to be a good Christian. He wanted to feel only love for people, wanted to keep his mind pure and high and turned towards God. He wanted to do the things that God wanted him to do, wanted to keep his heart open to know what those things were. His father didn't go to church with them. His father didn't believe in God. Gabriel asked him once, and only once, Dad, what do you think happens when we die?

Nothing, his father said. Nothing *happens*, and he smiled strangely, laughing a little. So don't worry about it. There's a bullet with your name on it out there, but you don't know when it's coming, so there's no point worrying about it. He never forgot what his father said.

Gabriel watched his father work and wondered how he could believe in nothing. Nothing. What was nothing? His mind tried to see it. He closed his eyes. Dark. That was nothing. But he could still hear. He tried to imagine not hearing. Silence. That was nothing. Darkness and silence, that's nothing. Yet, that was something, too, darkness and silence. He realized he was missing something, even though there was a part of him that knew from that day, that first day, that first real memory when he opened the basement door and saw the sun above and felt, knowing, how he'd come from there. That might be nothing. Going back would be nothing, but not the kind of nothing he was thinking about, now. So what was the difference? And what did his father mean? He couldn't understand what his father believed, but he didn't want to ask for an explanation because his father, like his sister, had a way of laughing, of shaking the head as though the question were too stupid to think about. Don't worry about it. That was all he knew, but how could he not worry about it? What about God? He held his cross, thinking over and over the word nothing, nothing, nothing until it was only sound.

Gabriel drifted through the recess chaos of the schoolyard, the tag games, kickball, clusters of kids and others running, the seagulls overhead, smoke from the incinerator, and Mark Tunney by the brick wall, outcast in filthy clothes with dirty hair and dirt under long, split fingernails. He was a violent boy. Gabriel overheard the teacher say once, prone to outbursts. He was frequently disciplined. They called him the Detention King. Most children were afraid of him, and he had no real friends as far as Gabriel knew. He was intently running a toy tank along the wall, making shooting sounds and playing out a private little war, and in a moment of calm observation, Gabriel thought he saw Mark Tunney's life like a documentary dream unveiling in a flash of sad apartments, lost jobs and eventually a tent alone in the woods. He went over to Mark and said, What kind of tank is that?

It's a Panzer, Mark said, and he kept on playing, making the sounds of war.

Can I see it?

Mark stopped and handed it to him and stood facing him like at any moment he would take it back. Gabriel held the tank in his hand. It was heavy, made of metal and had been hand painted with jungle camouflage of light brown and green paint. He gave it back and said, Nice.

You can have it, Mark said, and he handed it back to Gabriel. Gabriel held it in his hand again.

Really?

Sure.

Gabriel thought about it for a moment, and then said, No, that's all right.

I don't want it anymore.

Are you sure?

Yeah, take it.

Okay. Gabriel pushed it along the wall with its rubber treads rolling and made his own war sounds.

Say, Mark said, you want to come by my house after school? I've got a bike ramp. We can jump our bikes. Gabriel felt a tingling unease, as though he were being pulled into something, a friendship he was not sure he wanted. But he was holding the tank. He said, I'll have to ask my mom.

Okay.

They played more or less together but said nothing, on the edge of things where the grime gathered along the edge of the fence and the shadow of the old building opened its purse of moth memories that looked like radiation imprints on the cement. Then the noon whistle sounded with its piercing lament and unheeded warning of bombs and death, and all the children on the playground flapped their hands over their ears or ran or raised their voices to match the wail. Then recess was over, and they went back into class.

On the cover of his Scholastic Book Club book two people in white fur were wrestling a mastodon down with rope. The land was blue-white snow. Maybe he would read this one all the way through. Gabriel went down the list of vocabulary words, some simple, some a mystery. Magic words, things unknown. A spider in the corner of the window sat motionless in its web and had been and would be and budged not in a lifetime from its spot. The rain slid down the windows and the clock seemed to stop for a moment, second hand jumping backwards it looked like, then it started moving forward again. Was it a mechanical glitch or time cracking its knuckles? Why everyday did they sink and get stuck in the time eddies of the afternoon? His stomach boiled with a sense of dread. Why did he approach Mark Tunney? He was not sure now that he wanted to go over to his house, but the tank in his pocket had the weight of obligation in it. It was a transaction, now, a promise partially fulfilled.

When school ended he stayed back in the classroom. The other kids went on. He was afraid Mark might wait for him, so he lingered until he saw the other through the tall, warped classroom windows as he crossed the playground. Good spy work, Gabriel thought. Stealth lit the net of his brain. Gabriel went out and kept hidden in the ranks of other children filing out of school. This was the trick of invisibility. He even took the next street over for his way home so that he wouldn't accidentally catch up to the other or be seen by him.

When he got home, he closed the door behind him and looked out the window. He was going to wait out the afternoon but realized that the next day would mean facing the other and then having to lie because his mother wasn't even home and wouldn't mind or even know if he went for a bike ride or to play at a friend's house. He didn't want to lie to his mother about it. Nor did he want to have to make up lies to avoid the other. Quite a tricky corner here they lived on. Cross that street and you enter Laurelhurst, which meant the right to belong to the beach club! The diving tower! He had only ever been there as a guest. On this side of the street, however, what was it?

Less? Sand Point? That didn't seem right, but there was a difference. It made the hair on your arms crackle. Their house was once a farm-house with apple orchards all around. A few trees remained, but in the fog they looked like they went on forever. Maybe this was limbo. Even with ghosts in the walls their house felt like a blue-blood mansion.

He took his bike from under the porch and rode down the driveway and out onto the sidewalk. He rode around the corner and east on 47th Street past the Ford house and the other homes that all knew decent lives within. He rode around to the other side of the block, a short distance all in all, and then he was coasting up in front of Mark's house, where Mark was already carrying bricks out to the sidewalk. Gabriel stopped and stood straddling his bike.

Come on, Mark said. Are you going to help or what?

The Tunney house was distinct on the block with a grassless front yard worn flat and hard-pack smooth with dirt as fine as dust that floated up in occasional breezes. The paint on the house had faded away entirely, leaving the siding gray and weathered, blasted by wind and sun to a chance art warp of wood grain. The side yard and driveway were a dumping ground of old appliances and loose wood stacks and car parts and car carcasses and downspouts fallen from the eaves and lying where they landed. Quince trees grew in wild profu-sion, and willows and maples wove into each other with limbs that snagged papers and bags and balloons and whatever blew into their webbing. It was a place of long, slow and perpetual ruin, and the family moved through the neighborhood with the glaring shame and viciousness of untouchables.

Sure, Gabriel said, and he laid down his bike and followed Mark around the side of the house to the back. An enormous mound of bricks stood beside the garage. The garage itself could no longer hold a car, overflowing as it was with old chairs and appliances and boxes and planter pots and clothes and broken toys and bikes and tires. Gabriel stood for a moment in amazement, looking at the mountain of debris.

Here, you can carry them in your shirt, Mark said. You can get more that way. He pulled his shirt out and held the bottom edge with one hand as he lay bricks into its loom. Gabriel went over and pulled his shirt out and began to do the same thing. They carried the bricks to the front and put them down in a row along the sidewalk. They made two more trips and then had enough for a knee-high rise.

Come on, let's get the ramp, Mark said. He ran and Gabriel followed. They carried the plywood ramp out and put it on the bricks and stood back. Mark stepped onto it and rocked back and forth to see if it would hold and it did, then he laughed and jumped on his bike. I'll go first, he shouted, and he rode his bike back down the street and turned around and stood there for a moment twisting his hands on the handlebars while making engine-revving sounds. Then he rode fast up the sidewalk, his head bobbing up and down as he peddled. He hit the ramp, rose and shrieked and flew a bike-length before he came back down and skidded sideways to a halt. Yeeoww! he cried, and he turned to Gabriel and said, Now you try!

Gabriel climbed on his bike and rode back down the same stretch of sidewalk. He turned and rode back, accelerating, heading straight for the ramp. And then he hit the ramp and rose. He held there aloft for a moment flying forward neither breathing nor thinking, then came down hard on the front wheel and wobbled but maintained control. All right, Mark shouted. Gabriel smiled and turned his bike around.

They made several more jumps, and now Gabriel was getting a feel for it, how to pull back and keep the front up and come down on the back wheel in a smooth landing. Then Mark said, Let's make it higher.

All right, Gabriel said. He would admit no fear.

Hey, Mark said, Follow me.

Gabriel followed him across the dirt yard and into the house through the front door. A television glowed in the dark living room. The windows were covered with sheets, the couch and chairs covered with dirty sheets, the walls black to the height of the dogs that lay on the floor at the feet of a girl who sat on the couch watching TV. She neither spoke nor looked at them as they passed through the room. The kitchen was another matter, with dirty dishes on the counter and piled in the sink, garbage bags overflowing on the floor. It didn't feel like the kind of space where food belonged. Mark opened the refrigerator and took out a package of bologna and yanked out a round and offered one to Gabriel.

I'm not really hungry, Gabriel said.

They went out through the kitchen door into the backyard, and Gabriel went to the pile of bricks and began to collect another load. Mark stood in the driveway, dangling the bologna over his mouth. Then Gabriel saw an older boy standing in the back doorway. He stood with his arms crossed, leaning on the door jamb and watching Mark, watching Gabriel. Gabriel felt cool electric danger and averted his eyes and continued to gather bricks. When he had filled his shirt, he stood up and saw the older boy step forward and lift his arm and throw something that flashed quickly. Mark's hand jerked up and the metal wrench the older boy had thrown clattered on the ground followed almost instantly by the slap of the bologna on the cement. Mark dropped to his knees and began to scream. The older boy stood on the back porch laughing. Gabriel did not move.

That was a kind of laughter Gabriel had never heard before, and as he watched the older boy his head began to buzz and he saw a wave of movie-like images of the older boy's life rushing by as a flash of forced marching then a camp by a river, confinement in a small room, then back to the present moment with a sound like an airlock closing. Then a huge woman in a billowing yellow dress appeared. She must have been their mother, Gabriel thought, though he hadn't met her and wasn't even aware she was around, as she grabbed the older boy and pulled him back inside the house. Mark was still on his knees, cradling his hand and sobbing. Gabriel dropped the bricks and went over to him. Are you all right?

Mark's face was streaked with his tears, and he rocked back and forth but didn't answer. Gabriel stood there, not knowing what to do. Then a strange sound came out of the house, a slow, rhythmic thumping, like a washing machine off balance. Mark rose and wiped his face and went up to the back door and peered in. Still clutching his hand against his chest, he began to laugh, and it was the same as the older boy's laugh. He looked over at Gabriel and said, Come see this.

Gabriel approached. It was all a slow dreaming. The sound of the thumping and Mark's laughter mixed with the adrenaline shot from witnessing that violence only a moment ago and the bicycle jumps before that and all of it worked itself into a nausea boiling in Gabriel's stomach. Evening light rolled in a sepia wave of unreality as Gabriel stepped onto the porch and stood there beside Mark as Mark backed away slightly, allowing Gabriel to move in front of him and peer into the house. One of the big black dogs lay panting on the kitchen floor. On the other side of the room, the mother held the older boy by the hair and was slamming his head into the wall.

Gabriel pulled away. Mark moved back into the doorway, watching and laughing. Somehow, he had retrieved his piece of bologna and was eating it.

I gotta get going, Gabriel said, and he went around to the front of the house and picked up his bike and climbed on and rode fast for home.

Summer stretches out in long shadow hours with cobalt light burning late into the night sky through the trees. Even the avenues seem to telescope so there is no end. Gabriel rode his bike alone through the illuminated and mostly empty streets, past mystery homes with their doors still wide open because no one used their locks. The smell of the blackberries richly fused into the scent of sweet wisteria and the warm currents of pine air as he rode, awake and alive to the ends of his hair, coasting through the paths of Evergreen Park, crunching over horse chestnut shells, cruising around the baseball diamond and kicking up dust with his bike tires, then back down the overpass to the school and through the empty playground with chains tingtinging against the iron poles with tether balls removed, and then back along the street to his home, old farmhouse back among trees like none other in the neighborhood having been planted by the son of the former owner, a botanist, fond of Indian spruce and yew trees along with local camellias and rhododendrons and the robin-intoxicating ash.

He dropped his bike by the side of the house and went in and up the split stairs, one set heading down to the basement, the other up to the door to the hallway between the kitchen and the living room. Sound of a television, his father watching a baseball game. His mother talking on the phone. His sister alone upstairs in her room reading so fiercely he could hear the pages turn. This is everyday of their lives. This is how he remembers it forever. He moves through the hall and his mother smiles and reaches out and touches his arm. He falls into her for a moment, feeling the warmth of her body, feeling the vibration of her voice as she talks. She likes to sit in a little nook in the hallway between the kitchen and the living room under a square-framed spot in the wall where an old telephone still hung, the kind with an earphone and a mouthpiece and the crank you turned to dial up the operator. Sometimes, he could pick up the receiver and hear a thousand voices. Sometimes it just hissed. He knew the number by heart, there on a yellowed block of paper under the handset, and would know it the rest of his life, LA2-6217. What did the letters mean?

He went past the living room and the smell of his father's cigarette smoke. He looked in and saw his father in the chair in front of the television set. The lights were out. His father was smoking and drinking a beer. The sound was down on the television and the radio was on, playing a popular Mexican song. He studied his father for a moment, then moved in and stood beside him in the glow of the television screen. His father saw him and grinned and said, Hey, buddy. Then he nodded his head to the music and squinted. I love this song, his father said. Don't you love this song?

Yeah.

His father was funny, happier than he usually was, and his eyes burned with a dark joy. He reached over and patted Gabriel on the chest and said, Ah, my son, my son, as if this were a powerful thought to him. And then he felt the cross that Gabriel wore and picked it up in his hand and looked closely at it and said, Why are you wearing this?

I got it for being in the choir.

I know, but what does it mean to you?

I don't know. God. Jesus. Love.

Love? And he started to laugh, then stopped as if to check that he had heard right, Love? Gabriel said nothing.

Have they been teaching you the Bible at church?

Yes, some.

And what have they told you about God?

That God loves us all. That God is love.

Oh son, his father said, and he laughed again. You've got a lot to learn.

Like what?

About love.

What do you mean?

Nothing. You'll see. And that was all he said, and all he would say. It's getting past your bedtime, now get along. He leaned in and gave Gabriel a rough hug, and Gabriel knew that if he tried for more his father would snap.

Good night, Dad.

Good night, kid.

Gabriel went up the stairs, stepping between the loose molding strips with nails sticking out of them, a project half-finished for quite some time. The house was a series of unfinished projects, with painted samples on the walls with no decisions made yet and bare studs covered with clear plastic where walls would go. He climbed to the top floor and could see his sister, lying on her bed, reading. He went into his room and turned on the light. He walked the spiral path on the circular stitch rug, heel to toe, towards the center. From there, he leaped out onto the wood floor. He went to the open window and put his face close to the screen. Mosquitoes smelled him out and zoomed in. The stars blazed through the trees. The still air was full of crickets making their sounds. Others lived in this house and in this room, and he felt the heat of their lives at the window, details in the window sill, felt that those lives wanted him to remember, as though he were even now sorting through requests. The farmer didn't trust the banks and hid his money somewhere in the walls. When they first moved in, he and his sister went around tapping on the walls, listening for hollow spots, hidden treasure beneath every summer, every Christmas, every person he had ever met, things beyond his knowing, hazy-glimpsed and just out of reach yet still more real than the cool screen under his fingers or the mosquitoes trying to push through. He felt things moving around him that he could not actually see, and all of it glowed like a vague blueprint he could identify but not look at directly, the way his gaze went instead through the humming insect air into the kingdom of night.

If all games contain the idea of death, the gorge along the railroad tracks was full of inspiration. It's a kind of borderland, a peripheral zone. And war is the most popular game. There was an overpass beneath which they gathered, throwing rocks into the creek below, throwing rocks at the broken seats left from a train wreck and lying in the gravel and blackberries along the side of the tracks. They searched for bloodstains and thought they found some on the blue vinyl. They threw rocks at the passing freight trains then divided up with one group going over to the other side of the tracks and threw rocks at each other. Peter Andrews was a German soldier. It was a mystery why. No one else wanted to be German. He was their only expert on World War Two German military: the Stuka, the Panzer, the blitzkrieg, all laced with a smattering of scenes from *Weird War Tales*. He obsessed over the details of battles, and you'd think he was looking for someone he knew the way he absorbed wartime documentary shows on television, absorbing it all with the rapture of the last man on earth watching home movies. Walt McField was the opposite, more interested in setting up camp or pretending to sit through a lull in battle. He was an intermittent member of the crew anyway, often preferring house games with his sister's friends, but he was the only one who could get them into the beach club. Georgi had an accent and wore the same green jeans every day and had an old-world sense of fair play. He said with certainty that he was going to be a lawyer. They also converged in Georgi's garage because his parents were rarely home and he was richer than they were and had the newest stuff. Stuart lived next door to Gabriel. He was a small boy who was born premature and was thin-boned and wide-eyed and tentative. He preferred his own private world but came out if coaxed. He was a timid kid with a wolfish mother who, every time he left to play, said to him, Don't eat dirt, you'll get worms.

Across all seasons, they played war in the gorge by the railroad tracks. Until they discovered a new game: Chicken. It was not really a game so much as a trial. The name itself was the content of the rules, the goals, and the nature of its origin. It began on a hot Saturday. School was about to let out for summer. They all met in the gorge, and Georgi brought a rope. While they sat in the shade beneath the underpass, he tried to lasso things with it, throwing a loop out over signs, branches and saplings, catching nothing.

What are we going to do? Peter asked.

We could jump rope, Walt said. Peter sneered.

Come on, Walt, think.

Well, what do you think?

Let's tie it to two trees on either side of the tracks and when the train comes we'll see what happens.

Nah, said Georgi, That would just break it.

I've got an idea, Gabriel said, Let's tie it to a tree branch. We can make a swing.

That's a good one, Georgi said.

We can tie a stick to the end to sit on, Walt said. Or maybe a knot.

A board would be better, Georgi said.

They scrounged around and came up with a board and laid it against the tracks and stomped it down, snapping it into shorter pieces until they had a good length, then tied one end of the rope around it tight. Come on, Peter said, Let's find a good tree.

Hey, Georgi said, Over here. He climbed up the embankment and onto the cement overpass and went out about halfway and then leaned over and called down, Couple of you come give me a hand. Gabriel and Peter went up. Stuart and Walt watched from below. Hold onto my belt, Georgi said, and he leaned out from the overpass and tied the rope onto the lower bar of the railing while Peter and Gabriel held onto his belt to keep him from falling. And after he tied it, he shouted down, Go grab the end, Walt.

All right! Walt climbed halfway up the embankment as Georgi moved the rope back and forth, making it swing until Walt was able to reach out and grab it.

Got it! Walt shouted, holding it with one hand as he leaned back into the hillside. They had a swing.

All right! Peter said, and they scrambled down to where Walt stood holding the rope. Who goes first?

Georgi, definitely, Walt said. It's his rope.

Definitely Georgi. The others agreed.

Georgi took the rope and backed up the embankment as far as he could while keeping a hold on the rope. The others moved to the side. Georgi climbed onto the seat, pushed back with his legs, and went forward past them and out over the gorge. He made it to the other side, pushed off and came back and landed perfectly on his feet. He was breathing hard as he took another step back and launched out again and this time cried out, Yeaaaaah! as he swung out over the gorge and the railroad tracks to the other side and back again.

They each went in turn and the rope held up and the board held up and it was the greatest game of all. Time dissolved the afternoon. The sunlight retreated from the gorge until it came only in dusty rays through the lower branches and created a triangle of illuminated space beneath the overpass. And then they heard the train coming.

Peter was the last to swing across and come back to the bank and jump down and hold the rope, and they waited as the train came through. As it passed, they stood on the embankment and watched with wide eyes and laughter and terror, looking at each other and the passing cars and the obvious intersection of the ropeswing's trajectory and the path of the train. And so the real game was born.

How high was it? Georgi leaned out, with Gabriel and Peter holding onto his belt, while Stuart and Walt stood on the embankment and eyeballed the level of the seat.

A little higher, Walt said.

Not too high, Peter shouted. Don't be a chicken shit. He was the only one of them who really swore.

That looks right to me.

Me too, Stuart said.

And so the new level was set. It was harder to get on the swing, but the trajectory was now just above the top of the train, at least that was how they planned it, but someone would have to test it.

I think Georgi should go first again, Peter said.

Sure, now, Gabriel said.

Yeah, Peter, you wanted to go first before, Walt said.

All right, I'll go first.

Then you're first, Georgi said.

Peter climbed on and swung out. The arc was short and fast, but he was unable to get his footing again after he pushed off from the other side and came back. So he swung himself back towards the other side again but was either afraid or unable or who knows what, but he couldn't jump down on the other side either and ended up dangling in the middle. Ahh! he said, I'm stuck.

You're going to have to jump, Georgi shouted.

Peter leaned into the rope and tried to sway it back again and forced it into a small arc and then jumped off and fell onto his side on the embankment.

You all right? They were all asking as he rose from the dirt.

Yeah. He stood up and grabbed his shoulder and sat down on the dirt and winced, but he was all right. The rope swing settled straight again in the middle of the gorge and hung there out of reach.

Now how are we going to get the rope? Walt said.

Go up onto the overpass and push it, Gabriel said.

Look around for a long stick, Georgi said. And they looked around until Stuart found a long, dead branch. Georgi used it to guide the rope back into the hillside where Gabriel took hold of it.

I'm going to give it a try, Gabriel said, and he pulled the rope back and prepared to climb on.

You gotta push off hard, Peter said.

Gabriel held tight to the rope with both hands and jumped onto the seat and swung out fast through the strobes of light. He was back on the other side again in a quick return, but he wasn't able to get his footing, either. Before he swayed to a stop, he used his body to put the rope into a harder swing, leaning back and forth, pushing for extension, but all he could do was get the tips of his shoes to scrape the hillside, nothing that would make for a solid landing, and he realized he had to jump, too. He tried to get his body turned around so that he was facing the opposite embankment, that way he could drop off and turn and possibly land on his feet. When he got the best height he was going to get, he dropped off and fell onto his back with a thud that knocked the wind out of him. He lay frozen, unable to take a breath. The others encircled him, laughing and grimacing and shouting down into his face, Are you okay?

He was finally able to gasp and breathe and rise to a sitting position.

Who's next? Peter said.

Georgi went next, and he swung to the other side and pushed off again and was agile enough to jump just right and land on his feet and only had to drop to his knees and brace himself with his hands. Walt went next, and he too fell. Then it was Stuart's turn. But he didn't want to go.

Come on, Peter said. We all went.

He doesn't have to, Georgi said.

Yeah, man, Gabriel said. He doesn't have to go.

Then he's a chicken.

That's so stupid, Walt said.

It's the name of the game!

I'll go, Stuart said.

Right on, Stuart! And Peter grinned with his mean victory.

Stuart took the rope from Georgi and climbed to a spot higher on the hillside. Then he leaned back and swung out, but when he brought his legs up to throw them over the board, he knocked the board sideways. Then, he slid down as the rope went forward, and the force of his weight made his grip slip so that he was barely hanging on with the board pushed up under his arms. He struggled to pull himself up but couldn't get back onto the board. Ahh, he shouted, help me out! The rest of them scattered on the bank beneath him, calling out directions.

Pull yourself up, Georgi said.

Yeah, get on the board, Peter shouted.

I can't, Stuart said, and gradually the movement of the rope slowed, arc by diminishing arc, until he hung straight over the tracks. The drop was a long way, enough that they all knew it would probably mean a broken ankle.

Help, get help, he cried.

You gotta swing yourself over to the side, Georgi said.

Can you get it swinging again? Gabriel said. Use your body. Then you can jump onto the slope!

I can't. Get help, Stuart said.

You've just gotta swing a little way, Georgi said. And then you can drop off.

Then Stuart let out an animal scream in which they heard, I caaaan't. And then he started to cry.

We've got to get help, Walt said. I'll go for help.

Come on, Georgi said. Maybe we can swing him from above. Georgi went up the hill first, followed by Walt and Gabriel and then Peter. When they were on the overpass, Georgi leaned out while the others held his belt, and he began to push the rope back and forth, trying to move it towards the embankments. But below, Stuart screamed, Stop! Stop! You're going to make me fall. That's making me fall. Stop!

Try to hold on, Georgi said. We'll get you over to the side and you can drop off. It'll be easy, you'll see.

Noooooo! And Stuart let out another scream followed by sobs, so Georgi let go of the rope, and it gradually settled back, straight and still.

And then they heard the train.

Stuart, the train is coming, Georgi said. Let me swing you to the side. Stuart didn't answer. Georgi called down, Stuart, the train's coming. You've gotta let go. Gabriel and Walt and Peter looked at each other, then they all began calling down to Stuart.

The train's coming!

Let go.

Drop down.

The train's coming!

Stuart!

Let go.

Come on, drop down.

But Stuart didn't say a word. He clung to the rope, rigid, not even sobbing now but whispering with his face pressed between his arms.

Stuart!

The sound of the train was growing, coming from somewhere up the tracks on the other side of the overpass. Stuart clung to the rope, lit in the banded rays of sunlight shooting through the trees.

Stuart!

Let go!

Stuart!

And then the train appeared, coming through the sunlight. Perhaps the driver saw Stuart but didn't believe it. Perhaps Stuart's form was buried in the shadows and so invisible. Stuart! When the train swept under the overpass they all ran back to the edge of the slope and looked down. Stuart never moved. And then he was just gone. They watched, waiting. It was too unreal. And they said nothing while the train went beneath them, the ground trembling with its passing, while the wooden board tied to the end of the rope bounced along the top of the boxcars.

A BOUNDED RATIONALITY

When he enters in, the bar is comfortable darkness. The street outside is still a boiling mass of deconstruction, torn holes, exposed piping, transit lines and roofless underground rooms with bone fragments and empty eye sockets looking up, but all of it retreats in a world snuffed out as the doors swing closed behind him with a sound like an intake of breath, and he makes his way to the end of the bar where he usually sits and sits now again and nods to Hal who smiles and says, Hey, Jones, how ya doin?

Alive and kicking, mostly kicking, Jones says.

The usual?

Certainly.

And it appears before him delivered from Hal's hand, a perfect glass of liquid oxygen from which he drinks and becomes once again a wholly civilized human creature. He nods to Hal for another, and Hal already has it made.

Then he has another. And he doesn't speak to anyone, though the bar is a brew of noisy drunk conversations flowing across a conflagration of tongues, a babble of the Byzantines. They are rolling in from after work, sliding in and out of their lives. After the first two drinks, thoughts about the job sink, and he hovers now in the hazy chambers of quiet laughter, though he may have said out loud, The job hates to lose its grip and keeps a finger hooked around the rope of nerves at the base of the brain because the job reveals the designer at one remove that keeps a hold, and only through great theatrical measures or this gentlest revelatory libation can one escape that grip, but the brain has a lower register of banners and ticker tape with repeating messages like all aboard or abandon ship. He took another drink. Now, in his breath, in his heart, in his free flying mind, he achieves liberty.

She is slender and her hair black shines luminous negative space, a piece of the obsidian all. He thinks this as he soldiers on to another round, that this beauty is a kind of force burning through the material of dress, skin. Energy is rising up from its mysterious depths we will never behold entirely in this lifetime, halve it down as you may, and it is coiling and curling up inside this shape of strangeness. She is with another woman who has her back to him. He tries not to stare. It's not her in particular but the dark enigma of her hair. He has just enough ground to realize he is two drinks or so beyond the ability to engage in a light and playful way, that if he were to speak now his voice would come out through partially disconnected and excessively loud circuitry, thought moving faster than words like gold fire under its peeled-back casing. And from this velocity he has an ability he would not otherwise have to perceive that terrible beauty springing up blob-black as if whole chunks of the stage setting were removed or heady heads were pushing through, a movie moment among apes in a wonder before a mystery, even if he cannot touch it or communicate in the least groping, elemental way with it.

He has another. His fingertips are cold with it. But the dark enigma resists a direct approach. Now he is on the rise. The ground is shifting. There is an electric field everywhere he looks crackling with its charge. Sometimes the noise comes from his skin or from under the skin. When he moves his head quickly, everything breaks up into particles. You could put your hand in the space between the orbiting thoughts these heads exude if you only had a hand. Imagine pulling back the skin of time. Everything reassembles. Stillness is a stance. In the stopped moment the seams glow with blue stitches.

Someone appears, a young man laughing. He is warped youth and veiled menace and dives into Jones's vicinity with a slur of editorials that come out like garbled incantation, bizarre and meaningless, with words that sound something like Halomonomon, lokiter ronmolalam. Roat? Roat? Then he splits with laughter, and Jones realizes that in the reality he has dislodged himself from, the black-haired woman has shed some essence-revealing reptilian rider with scaled cheeks and bronze shimmering eyes and mouth puckering and sucking and smacking wet sphincter Who? Who? Oh. She is the octopus inking the waves.

Jones turns away and then turns back again and the creature is only woman now. He rises from his place and signals in that simple way that looks like a blessing and pays for his drinks. Haven't I been through enough? He lunges half a league onward. The crowd folds its human wave behind him, opening again and more before him. Strangers lean in with teeth gleaming and eyes blinking and laughter voices mingling, and he smiles, he thinks, as he moves through the funhouse mirror scene.

Through the door the world howls. Cranes. Jackhammers. The cardiac beeping of trucks in reverse. Steam. A demon from above dropping a yellow wobbling egg sack from its dripping mucoidal pouch. Like sightseeing in another's nightmare. The moon offers its own distractions.

He staggers on and lets his body drive. He seeks the bus numbers on the bus stop post, the tiny script of arrivals. People are waiting with bored regard and homefire stares. Others are standing in groups by the soup kitchen under the overpass across the street. Others are emerging from the ground with wet limbs and tendril hair, broken shells still clinging to the skin on their backs. Someone takes him by the arm, a woman, her face burning through the halo of her hair. Are you going to go to the party?

I don't think I was invited.

He is standing in a doorway. The automatic doors open and close and open and close. Move on, buddy, someone shouts from a bright distance, a row of cashiers, rows of shelves stocked with things things things.

He careens off of something. Watch it! he hears.

The streetlights burn and waver and circle each other in furious veronicas with flames inside of flames that sputter and flare. Olé! Rain is falling, and he feels it soaking through the shoulders of his coat. The neon lights of the Market are bleeding across the bricks and the black asphalt and the dark crowds coming from everywhere.

The bus arrives and he climbs aboard. Then the bus moves and he quick-steps down the aisle, a voice loud saying, Congregations of The Dead, as face after face turns away and he fleeting realizes he is the only one here. He collapses into an open seat. The bus is hot. He is soaked and steaming. I am made of steam, he hisses. He laughs and melts against the window. The sky is a shimmering of undersea eyes, primary colors of red, green, and yellow. He shuts his eyes and spins and spirals into white falling into black and out.

Jones knew trends. That was his gift. He made his clients money and called himself a seer. That was his curse, too. Never invest based on a hunch, at least that's what he told the clients. He wasn't poring over numbers, either. Horses stomping on a spreadsheet were more accurate than an army of accountants. But that's not what profit was about. Any fool could read the news, the charts, price index, anticipate the acquisitions and the mergers. Any fool could buy low, sell high. That wasn't the game, either. That was a Mickey Mouse version of the long game and a purgatory for numbers people, and he had never met a numbers person who knew how to find the living wire, who had any grace or charisma at all, who could lead anyone into the zone. Money, and he never told the client this, money never beats grace and charisma, yet grace and charisma get you into the zone. It was important that the client believe first and foremost in the charm, and like a hypnotist with a swaying watch he put them on track, cultivated their portfolios, taught them how to spend and acquire but even more so, and this was his secret pedagogy, how to live. Once locked into that trajectory, all the gears mesh.

When Mrs. Breen's husband died, she was living like a servant. Mr. Breen was a tightwad penny licker who lived embedded in the hum of machines, an expanding chain of laundry shops which brought in more money than he knew what to do with. Actually, he did know what to do with it, meaning growth: he built more shops. That was the only way he could think, he was a feeding organism. He was more like a machine himself, and yet he was rich, yes richer than a king. But Mrs. Breen never knew this, or if she did she didn't realize it, because they lived in a simple house under the water tower and a thrumming transformer with a watershed for a backyard and convinced themselves that they were simple country folk. When he died, quick as a rush job, his heart stopping on its last key-code digit, she had no idea how much the business was worth, how much someone would be willing to pay for it, since she had no knowledge or ability or desire to run it herself. But when she found out, the pain of her loss shifted quickly, and a kind of quizzical resentment rose in its place. That was the moment he knew she was someone who could learn to actualize her full potential as a being of grace, and he would show her the way.

After that she went to Europe—twice. Then China walked the Great Wall. She brought home pictures of herself beneath the open arms of Christ the Redeemer in Rio de Janeiro. And she now hosted the largest collection of glass art in the Northwest, housed in a clifftop home with high ceilings and thick blond pine beams, overlooking the Sound and the Olympics and the city itself. He didn't really agree with her taste in art, but it wasn't for him to judge her way of living, only push her through the door of living it. She was an art lover, now, and that was the point, that was all that mattered. And she trusted him entirely with the estate of her financial affairs. He managed money for her, and by this she in turn made money for him, and they were both happy and they never spoke of the courser matters of number amounts, nor where her streams of income went on some occasions and how those little journeys didn't have to show up on official records but could blossom in ways that made both their lives blush. In fact, if she ever did try to bring up the issue of actual amounts and accounts, where they were and how they were invested and how they were doing, he carefully guided her back, like a lighthouse beacon, from the dangerous rocks of financial scrutiny. He did this most often by raising the image of her dead husband like a skull pulled from the grave and hung before her as a warning, as if to say, see, this could be you too if you become too curious about and distracted by the matter of numbers.

Yes, Mrs. Breen had blossomed. He considered her a friend, even a kind of protégé. And there was Mrs. Andrews and Mrs. Kline and Mrs. Woodruff. Most of his clients were women, it was true, but not because he primarily sought them out more as a protector in a time of extreme vulnerability during which a more unscrupulous person might take advantage, but because he found in women an aesthetic he enjoyed so much in himself, a sense of taste, a feeling for refinement, and an ability to learn. Not all of course. There were those who had to be involved if not in charge of the intimate details of their money. They couldn't help themselves. This was the frontier, after all. But with these, he simply could not work. An artist, after all, must not be hobbled by the scrutiny and questions and good-intentioned input of the audience. It had to be a harmonious relationship, a trusting relationship, a relationship which found its shape and motivation in a feeling for life.

The truth was, he rarely attended to the details himself. He had to be acutely cautious not to become a sacrifice to the same hazards he warned his clients away from. That was the job of the accountant and the broker, and they were inclined to this kind of work and performed their functions well with the assistance of their avatars. His job was to cultivate relationships, to be in the right place at the right time, to troll the culture for its active energy spots and then to siphon off the overlooked abscess here and there and charge them with his own kind of magic. In order to do this, he had developed his ears. He carefully culled information such as who was replacing who as a marketing manager, what ideas they held onto, who had capital backing up and underappreciated, who was starting up a new venture, and always who was coming and going from this world, and this information he fed into the system of his virtual calculator. That was the legitimate part. It was that simple, really. He absorbed information and siphoned it through the baleen of his creativity and let the numbers incept the way they naturally would. Not that everything hit. There were losses, too. There were always losses. But even losses had value accountants and tax lawyers could leverage. Losses were part of the general and obvious game, a necessity nearly, and unless they completely decimated the principal, those losses were not matters for concern or conversation and could rightly be viewed as the inevitable systolic signature of an investment in life. The key to winning was to simply keep playing. Play the strength when you found it, stay close to the hot spots. When a person or a company goes cold, move on. And that was just what he did. Sometimes he lost relationships this way, even ones that seemed like they were based on the most deeply rooted common values. Nothing remains static. Yet, if these friendships did not last, then they simply weren't meant to be. Letting go is the traveler's secret weapon.

Yet within this perfectly artful system, there were times when it was simply a job. How did this happen? It had little to do with the numbers or the success or failure of investments. That was the smallest actual concern and focus of the job. It came in the contact with the people. As beautiful as these relationships were, they were still, as much as he tried to deny it, based on business. And because of this, he maintained a mask. He had to give so much of himself in the cultivation of these relationships that when the chance to actually be alone arose, he often faced a wall of exhaustion and lay stone still on the floor of his office or home, unable to move, plastered to the bottom of the sea as the black clouds coiled above him. These were dark, black flag times. These were the sinkholes, the despair spots, the wasted, drained-out husk depressions that were almost insurmountable. Moments when his job displayed itself as what it was: a job. And that could feel unbearable. A drink or two would sometimes help. Three or four were often necessary to regain a necessary balance.

In fact, he did some of his best work drunk, particularly if the client was drinking with him. Those could be true moments of inspiration and friendship, as he liked to believe it, the spirit punching through. Mrs. Andrews had a wonderful sense of humor and drama, even if she was sometimes demanding. She was a showrunner, but recently she told him the harrowing story of her son who apparently witnessed another boy's death when they had been playing near some train tracks and the boy was struck and killed instantly. My god, Jones said when she told him this, that's absolutely tragic! We must have another drink.

His own finances were, alas, a shambles. He had personally invested money his wife had inherited into an upstart venture, but a digital coup annihilated that venture. Some disasters can't be anticipated. It had its eroding effect on the relationship, and then she targeted what she thought were his obvious weaknesses. The war of attrition raged on. She could not accept his drinking or the demands of his work, and so finally divorced him. It was inevitable, he now thought. The dividends were diminishing. Her first husband had drowned, leaving her with two children alone. Yet that first husband still haunted the house, his picture hanging in the hallway, and she refused to take it down. The children never warmed to him. In fact, they were downright hostile. The boy, who was older, would only call him by his first name and regarded him with the glare of a rival gorilla. The girl was quiet and sweet in her way. But he watched as her mother tried whittling down her personality by passing on in some blind and aggressive way the shame of their father's death, saying things like, Well, if you act like that, you know, people will only say it is because you don't have a father.

Relationships. He was not born to succeed in them, himself, not romantic ones at least. He had the talent to create and initiate them, with the trajectory always tending towards his own detriment and eventual sorrow. He was born alone and lived alone and, well, his death was a daily meditation. How would it come? In a long slow sickness wasting away, deterioration and quiet, painful annihilation? Or in a sudden catastrophe? Or by his own hand? Or the quick and forgiving death of the worker whose heart one day explodes like a glorious nova? Each morning when he rose, like this one, and pulled himself from the catafalque of his own excesses, he wondered how death would visit him and what sort of warning, encouragement or insight it would give.

And so he climbed back into his skin, wretched, nauseous, sneezing, blear-eyed and dark in his mind, showered slowly and without resurrection, dressed in clothes that felt like sand paper on his inflamed flesh, and drank coffee as he gazed eastward through his living room window, the sun burning dull in a bank of grim gray clouds and the people of the neighborhood creeping germ-like from their homes. Good morning Mr. Jones.

A drink by mid-day, that's what he thought. I'll have a drink by mid-day. Just one. I'll go over to McCormick's and have one glass of wine and a little bite to eat. It will be refreshing. Constitutional. Invigorating and inspiring. It will be with a meal, so it's not really like drinking at all.

Russell, the hungry little toad and new man at the firm, was breathing down his neck. But Russell was a numbers man with no panache, no flair, and Jones knew this. No class, all clothes, cars and that nasty way of finishing people's sentences for them. Here he comes, all gloat and aftershave.

Hey, Jonesy, how're the little old ladies treating you? His teeth were large and white.

I suppose you've been trying to cover your losses from that dip on Friday, haven't you, Jones said.

I'm saying buy, buy, buy. It's bargain-basement Monday right now, buddy. Even the small fry can take a bite. Put the geris on it.

Jones thought: Russell never actually looks at you. He's always looking around for another place to be, another soul to suck. One drink by mid-day, Jones thought. One drink. He said, Ride out the wave, is that it, Russell? All illusions? Smoke and mirrors? Reality lies in the imagination and we're in it for the long haul? A snake biting its own tail? He lifted a collegial fist and noticed that it was shaking. Did Russell catch that?

Yeah, Russell snorted, right. And he was already moving away before the last word fell from his mouth.

One drink.

The office was a slow-motion newsreel with grainy paper cut-out figures curling up under the heat of their desk lamps. The nausea crested and fell. Jones kept his office door open, but just barely, so he wouldn't appear to be hiding or idling, which he was. Business, business, business. He read his messages. A meeting was scheduled for 2:30. Who meets at 2:30? People like Russell. One drink. And it will have to be just one.

He checked the updates on the trends, the recommendations, the hot sheet, but nothing caught his attention. Go where the gaze goes, out the window overlooking the sloping parking lot, the sinking ship as they call it. Its whole form glared sepulchral in the morning light. Everything glares. A large dump truck lumbered up the street and his office windows rattled from its passing. The light itself cut his eyes, and now this sound assaulting his ears. The window glass sagged, liquid and rippled with age. Breathe on it and all the faces of the room's occupants will appear. A brief wave of vertigo hit, slight throbbing in the arms, tingling in the hands, a copper taste on the tongue and that black spiral tip punching through the top of his head, but he kept to his feet. Passing out was not without its allure.

His account was heavy with old messages, the pulsing anxiety of clients who listen to the news and panic. He was waiting for another few hours for the stories to change. They always rise soon after a dip as the bottom feeders come in and the middle cruisers drift back in. After six percent, he'd make the calls, which would be nothing but hand-holding and reassurances. This has happened before, in various forms, from priest to legislator, keeping the calm was the art of leadership. The system always recovers. And so he waited, looking down through the office window at the rigging of spiderwebs laced over the city and the flying light vehicles, the particles and the traffic waves, klieg lights through the clouds and green searchlights strafing the streets with the sounds of sirens and foghorns and music, and he took a little flask from his desk drawer and took a sip and felt the warm flow of the Hippocrene that made his outline in the glass glow like a god moving effortlessly through the fabric of its creation.

Jones let out a vapor breath, turned and made his way up the backstairs and into the hallway and at last to his office where he collapsed in his high-backed leather chair and spun it around, throwing his feet up onto the window ledge. The sun was walking off on long shadow legs across the street. Traffic was already increasing. Cars flipped on their headlights. He reached back and turned on the radio. A little jazz would be just about right. Thelonious Monk emerged. Blue Monk, and it became a kind of soundtrack to the moment as he drifted and his breathing slowed until his eyes closed. The last thing he heard was an advertisement on the radio: that's right! We're giving it away. Once a year we do it, no strings attached! Just come on down to the showroom, this Saturday, and everyone will have a chance to win! What's the catch? There is no catch! All you have to do is show up! Put out your hand and keep to your feet! The person who lasts the longest wins, and we'll put you behind the seat of a new vehicle! So come on down! We'll be open as long as the party lasts! Don't be late! Only those who arrive between ten and noon will be eligible! So see ya down here!

A search for the grail, and everywhere he turned, the image of a hat flying off a head appeared to him: an acting company production billboard with the back of a man's head, his hat tumbling off (it happened to be a bowler) while one hand reached out for it; then a book cover of a faceless man, a hat rising from the top of his head (once again, a bowler) in magic levitation. Someone holding a newspaper, the headline reading: New Mexico Hat, seriously, and so forth, in fairly quick succession, as though a beam were shining the idea into his world in different versions of the basic image, showing up in various places and designs, meant to grab his attention like a cosmic advertisement. And being someone open to the symbols and suggestive images mind-at-large might offer up, yet he considered there were several possibilities. Images could be coming out of the universal whirlpool to tell him something specific, yes? Or, they're all nothing more than coincidental images which because of his attention become invested with significance. Or, mind on high alert was seeking some code to resolve a vague equation and in mixed surges and signals reaching out and engaging rational consciousness in the process. Or, he was simply a strong receiver? Big Mystery! So he noticed this, noted it, and lodged it in his mind for future consideration. Now if only I could find that folder…

It would have to wait. He was tired beyond comprehension, moving through a throng of foes leering with secret knowledge, as though aware of significant information meant for him but untransmittable at this time. He stood at the bus stop, his bus stop. Everything moved in slow motion. Cars flowed, dragging their afterimages behind them like diva furs. The people sitting in the restaurant on the second floor of the building across the street seemed to move with mechanical stops and starts, repeating their motions as if on a recorded animatronic loop. In the construction site, now quiet, canvas tarps rippled like galleon sails and stopped, catching momentarily like a strip of gray film stuck in invisible sprockets, a movie image rolling to a point and then stopping only to rerun again exactly as before, over and over.

The bus arrived. He climbed on board and slipped into the doldrums of its warm interior and pale lights. It leaped and rattled into the traffic, and he leaned his head into a bank of stars and drifted free from his mind.

PART TWO

THE PARIS CLUB

She awoke in the grainy dawn, the bus rattling with its velocity, and for a moment she had a vision of herself in a time long ago crossing the country and not for the first time in a wagon on a rutted road over this same landscape she was now traveling with its heat bands of prairie and sage scents and degrees of gray, and she was convinced by these impressions in the borderland that she had in fact lived that life and that it was only now resurfacing because such actions and ages lie indelible under the surface of the scenes we live through as she drew herself fully out of sleep.

Jack lifted his head, his eyes opening to hers. He smiled and said, Morning sunshine. He slid over and kissed her vigorously, then pulled himself up and stretched and squinted at the land outside swirling like dragon's breath.

Where do you suppose we are now? he said.

New Mexico? she said. Maybe Arizona?

Nah, not Arizona yet, he yawned, nodding. Then again, maybe so, he said. He leaned across her and shoved the window open and stuck out a hand and felt the outside. Dry, he said, and pulled his hand back in, letting it rest on her shoulder. So what do you say when we get into town you let me show you around? I've got some friends. You'll like them. They're real characters, and I mean that in an affectionate way.

I'll bet.

Really and truly. They're good people of the earth, better than your average trivia-night crowd. A little strange at times, maybe, but good-hearted. Old Francis Jones, he is my brother to the core! He was married, career and prospects and the whole bit. Last I heard he may have a kid. About as normal a person as you'd ever meet, we were in the cradle together.

Was married?

He got divorced a few years back, but he's better for it. Last I heard he had a little business of his own.

Doing what?

Oh, selling things people need to get rid of in a hurry.

Great, she said.

He smiled. I'm only kidding, he said, pulling his arm a little tighter around her shoulder. There are opportunities, you know, when things fall off the back of the truck. It's not like he's got watches hanging inside an overcoat. And then there's T-Bear. Sweet fella, Canadian, I think. And Piston. He's exactly how he sounds, too, full of piss and vinegar.

His name is Piston?

That's what people call him.

Why?

I don't know. He's a fireball, that's why. Always going. Kansas born and bred but way too much spark for that geography, so he ran outta there on energy you can't keep up with. You'll love him. You'll love all of them. They're like my family, which is better than family.

Where is your family? Your real family?

Well, now, that's a long story.

Well we don't seem to have any place special to go.

All right, then. Let's see now…well, to start with, I come from Utah. Yes, Utah and all that means. My father was…something about that part of the world…you might want to say he's crazy but crazy brilliant. Not the kind of crazy that would drive him to an asylum but the low creeping slithery snake kind, the kind you find in a revivalist preacher, which is what he was, the kind of insane you'd see in a man who fights with his god, can you believe that? Fighting with your god? Devoting yourself to this god and in a way hating that god and fighting against that god with your acts as if to say, All right, I'll do it, but just to spite you, to *make* you save my soul, and things like that he used to say late into the night, crazy nights so we thought he was drinking, my two brothers my sister and I, but he never drank. He was not a drinking man. No. But he was a man drunk on his religion, addicted to his faith. And I don't know all about this, but I don't think he was always somber, he burned. He scared people but not with the fear of hell. He didn't think anyone was going to hell. He didn't think hell was any place anywhere other than this, and he said it was within your power to live in hell or heaven right now, that the kingdom of god was upon us, meaning within us as well right now and not off in some fairyland future, and so he carried on conversations with the dead, with angels, demons, demigods... People came to see him and he would pray with them and summon up their dead relations and speak in their voices. Tissues and weeping. People would come with their ailments and the ailments of their brothers and mothers and children, and he'd go into a kind of trance, sometimes for hours in which he wouldn't say anything at all, then come out and say something like, you need to put the boy on a diet of vegetables and water, eliminate all meat, for now. His blood will respond. Or, you need to move north. Or, you need to shed all your leather. Or, you need to stay out of sunlight for the season. Or, spit on an onion and throw it as far as you can and bury it where it falls... things like that. And daily he prayed, but it was not the kind of prayer you might hear in a regular church. When he prayed he ranted. He would call his god to task for the things he considered unjust in this world, saying, All right now, Lord, there's this problem of sickness, a bad sickness in the people, and I'm doing what I can, but you've got to move their hearts, you've got to do your job, Lord, you've got to move them, move their heard hearts because these people are sick, Lord, lost in money, lost in gluttony, lost in the bloat of their knowledge, lost in fear, lost in lust, lost in want. And we don't need another divine prophet. We've got all the divine prophets we can use. We need you, Lord, to rise up in us, to burn brightly in our hearts. Now do it! This is no time to sit back and observe, no time to lay dormant, no time to be abstract and eastern. I'll do my part, Lord, but you've got to come to us, give us your fury, give us your love, give us your beauty and your strength and your grace and your power before we falter and it's too late. And if it is too late, well then Lord give us the vision to see clear into the next world, and don't let me live out my days in the realm of the dying and the suffering alone, come, come with your burning music. Or if I must, then give me the sign and I'll do my ministering in your place, but tell me, Lord, tell me now, now, do you hear? Now! Do it! And he would go into a fit of talking, words pouring out of him that were nothing like anything you've ever heard before but sound like words nevertheless, like something that should make sense but doesn't. He burned on the edges of his mind, on the edge of this world, and though he was never cruel or mean-spirited or unfair or unkind, we were afraid of him. Who wouldn't be with that kind of madness? We weren't the kind of family that went on trips to the Grand Canyon or the beach or the county fair. He was too on fire for anything like that. He was on a mission. And anytime we were out with him, people would approach him, whether they knew him or not, they would come up to him— they knew, they just knew, like some network informed them or they just saw it in his eyes or burning in his face, these filthy, homeless, sick, decrepit bastards, stinking foul and penniless creatures that could barely walk or talk, and they would zero in on him and take his arm or his hand, and he'd get into a clutch with them and nod with great earnestness and intensity like they were old friends, and he'd whisper in their ears, tell them secrets, things that made them jolt back and either smile or weep or sometimes just go into a daze but go away as if something had been sprung free inside their brains. And when we asked him what he said, he'd just say, I told them god's words, which we knew meant the words of his prayers, those weird, gobbledy sounding and a little scary words which made your skin crawl to hear them. In any other age he would have been burned as a heretic, I suppose. For sure in any other age they would have killed him.

Did you go to church?

We lived in his church. No other church would have him. He stormed out of churches in a fury, if we went at all, which after I was maybe eight years old we never did. He called them charlatans and papist fools and ignorant literalists and fiends. He said, You've got to see, you've got to see the beauty of the metaphor. If you can't see the beauty through the symbol, then you see nothing at all. You don't know God at all.

The beauty through the symbol, like the cross?

The cross, the church itself, the Passion, the whole thing. He said it was like a map, and you had to read it like one if you were going to find your way anywhere in this life. That's what all religions are, he said, and he could as easily find god through Buddhism or Islam or Zen or Shinto or Tao or anything, he knew them all. It just so happened that he was raised with the stories of the Bible mostly, all the way up to his own working days, so it was like as if he walked right out of those pages, and it was that language he'd learned to use to speak of his god.

That makes sense to me, she said.

But not to Utah. They ran us out of that state. Death threats. Hate mail. But that wouldn't have done it, I suppose, until somebody, a group of them, set fire to our house.

My God!

Ha! Maybe so! At that point we were desperate to go. That was when we came to California. Like a prospector of the spirit! And as my brothers and sister and I got old enough, we just split. We had to. Who could stay around something like that? It's like living near a volcano.

How old were you when you left?

Seventeen.

Where did you go?

I joined the Navy. Went all over the world. I never looked back. Discharged in San Francisco, but by then, well, by then...there was no going back. He continued his ministry, if you could call it that. Healing. Praying. Maybe it was all just a sham. He seemed to believe it, though, and I guess that's all you need.

Can you stop twitching? she said.

What, you mean my leg? His leg was jumping in the quick percussion of junkies and caffeine grinders. Oh, honey, that's the thoroughbred in me, I'm always on the race.

As if someone pinched their lips and turned their heads at the same time, they turned and looked through the window into a world not fully materialized, overcast and loaded now with something from his story, something leaching out of the telling and the father image, evoked by gaze and vision and narrowed-down to a swift and sudden appearance then a vanishing of a single bare dead-looking tree on fire in the middle of nowhere, a door through which to come and go, yet the land seemed still unformed at the borders with a gray haze of obscurity overall as the bus rolled and rumbled, the engine whining from something loose or off track inside, a deafening sound with a silence of its own, as they hurtled through the desert on a road that had no visible beginning or end with a few hills unfurling faint in distance, and the indeterminant middle space loaded with pyramids of eyes.

And so she had to assess now what she knew of him, this stranger on the bus. He was a jester walking upside down with one foot over the precipice. Everything coming out of his mouth was a mix of memory and imagination. She could see the bones in his neck like a living X-ray with his smile cantilevered like a bit of fabric loosely attached. They rode through the desert haze-dust slouching into a new incarnation. Wasn't this her life also? She made a mental defensive catalogue of the things in her bag, the clothes, the book which she hadn't read, the notebook she hadn't written in awaiting the next versions of herself, and the gun she hadn't yet had cause to use. What could she expect from this stranger or anyone? Trust? Trust in her, maybe? She was fully aware of the effect she had on people, how they saw her as the follower, the meek one who'll obey if pressed hard enough. She would play along. This new freedom was hers, and it wasn't to be taken even by this man, though everything in his manner seemed to suggest that he expected nothing less than a total devotion which he would never offer in return. The fool. A thought unbid steeled itself in her: hide me in your wing, O hide me in your wing. It was as if the words went out to her mother and as if her mother in fact heard her and was even now responding in ways she couldn't discern but felt like a low-grade fever.

The land wove itself around her and unwound itself in distance, as the man kept his arm around her and pulled her close and kissed her cheek and then her mouth. And the words kept coming like a voice inside her head as she felt his hand on the back of her neck, the words continuing even as he arched and groaned and the bus drove on and on.

It was the kind of place you'd never look at twice. Glance and counter glance of the crew lingering around the white stone steps under belaureled cornices and expressionless faces in windows and you'd pass by with head forward to avoid those eyes and the feral impulses behind them. The architecture is from no time in particular, and most likely some sacrifices occurred during its construction, ask the janitor who might tell you on a cigarette break of bodies buried in the foundation, moans in rooms no one will inhabit again. Identical windows of soot-begrimed glass enclosing a darkness past the reach of any Anasazi fire arrow or far-seeing eyes cut into the cliff face. And yet sunlight rides surface-changing the angles during the day to redesign its shadows in their geometries of who and whom smoking and planning a next move. Uniformity in the design breaks in a variation of voices, music, arguments, laughter and screams to coalesce in a single babble or howl emerging from the tenement heart. And you might have the same thoughts she had as she passed through a throng of loitering ghosts out front, one wrong move, gesture or word could turn the engine of the worst machinery, that thing dormant in everyone's fate-line that might be plucked depending on the individual soul or whims of Fortuna, life metrically arranged with details malleable as clouds.

Pass on through. The doors welcome with a ticket-taker's smile and plunge you into the funhouse. That's just how it appears. Pass on through the hubbub, the unwell and boiling underworld you thought you'd never sink to but always knew existed at the border of your dreaming, your darling. There is a familiar look of broken mirror institutions, of grade schools without heat, of lavatories and toilet cakes, of wet coats hanging on hooks, old shoes, food in paper bags, and the pervasive human smell of sweat and worry beneath ammonia cleanser, sparks of hospital memory, first smells, birth and of course decay and death. The floor is green linoleum, faded and rutted down the center from continuous walking, surrounded and permeated by a spray of black protozoan shapes that float and seem from the condition you take on when entering to writhe.

Doorways, filthy tee shirts peeling back from swollen bellies like burned skin, lurid smiles, missing teeth, little dogs, birds in cages. Pass on through. The eyes narrow to sleep but no sleep will come. Sleep no more. Not here. Here, now she'll keep most acutely vigilant.

Music. Television sets on tabletops. Stains on the walls. Carpets with tasseled corners. A coverless book. Doorway after doorway of little scenes she peers into but not for long, these fast tracking worlds within worlds of people changing to something else or come as something broken or stripped of layers and nuance or whatever, each world had its own dragon curled around treasure no one wants, one after another in a rush from nothing more than eye contact, to rise, rise from fetid abandonment and blaze.

She climbed the stairs not pulling back but not fully compliant as he drew her along holding her hand. And on the way she caught hints of hidden doorways showing up in various places in that untethered flowing of the family journey, fuzzy openings like exploding dandelions, doors that boiled and wobbled with electric fringe bolts and filmy green curtains of liquid air like mist in a spook house neither cold nor warm as she reached to touch and put her hand forward with fingertips going in and vanishing but feeling nothing because her circuitry made her yank her hand back fast. And just like a child learns not to touch a stove after one bad burn, she never reached again, nor mentioned seeing them to anyone, thinking that somehow saying what she saw would get her into trouble, following an old instinct that said the best thing to do in most situations was to be invisible.

They went to the room he had purchased and inside the smell hit her, the inherited smell of countless preceding occupants layered in the fabric of the chairs and the wood of the floor. She sat on the bed. He must have smelled it too because he said, Whoooweee, and went to the window to open it, wedging his hands up under the middle of the frame and pushing hard. It wouldn't budge. He banged at the casement and the glass rattled in its puttied frame. Damn thing, he said. He pushed at it again and it slid up and halted. He banged on it and knocked at it and got it to maybe three quarters of the way open, which allowed some air to flow in along with the horns and people and sirens and smoke and heat from the street below. Welcome.

He went around the room, turning on the lights, but when he came to one lamp, he twisted the switch and nothing happened. He tapped the lamp and tried the switch again and still nothing happened. He reached in and twisted the bulb and it flickered once but then out. He took it out and stood holding the dead bulb. But he didn't seem satisfied with this. He went to one of the other lamps and turned it off and reached in to unscrew the bulb, but it was hot and he jerked back his hand and said, Mother fu—! and bent down and looked at it as if looking at it would heal it, and waited and then licked his fingers and tried again and quick unscrewed it and pulled it out and tossed it on the bed and tried the bulb that was apparently dead in that lamp and once again it gave a tantalizing flicker of light but went out again, so he took it out and shook it by his ear and said, Filament must be broken. It was almost a silent comedy routine, watching him, and she felt a wave of warmth and affection for his domestic stumbling as he put the working bulb back into the lamp he'd taken it from and stood there with the half-dead bulb in his hand unsure what to do with it, as if he were thinking out loud that it obviously wasn't going to work but had enough life in it that it didn't make sense to throw it away, such was the depth of compassion and philosophy her newfound companion exhibited.

He put the bulb on a dresser and looked at it for a moment and smiled and shook his head.

She was surprised he had so many friends. They all descended, filling up the room en masse smoking and drinking and talking so fast and over each other she couldn't believe that anyone was following a single conversation. Rather in this braided connecting, she was ushered up and introduced to Quince with heavy beard and ripped up dress shirt with a rich dark oozing under the armpits. He kept a hard eye on her and winked with stale interest pulling back his lips on a smile of yellow canines. And here was T-Bear with eyes nearly shut yet one open slightly and in constant scan. He sat beside a gelatinous creature named Balel who smoked a long hash cigarette and laughed from the diaphragm beneath a platinum wig. And here was Piston, rapid talking bolt of a man with knee in constant jitter like his name, who smoked with such rapidity cigarettes shriveled between his fingers as he spoke and poked at people like he was jabbing them with an electric prod. Others came and went in the barrage and clatter and smoke clouds rolling, because everyone was smoking so much there was a perpetual blue unrealscape at eye level undulating and shifting with occasional heads poking through, talking and talking, all a rush and a jumble with a bottle going around and stinky joints and people shouting and laughing, rising to their feet to make a point like a parliament of cats, more and more coming and going so she was never sure who was really there at all, just the rush of talk and the ferocity of the words and the conviction behind them, like:

It's all economics, Piston was saying. A numbers game for the numbers people who get it. They get it and so they make shit happen.

Economics? T-Bear said, and from his tone he seemed skeptical. Maybe not about the concept, which wasn't clearly defined, but Piston's ability to formulate it.

Think about it, Piston said. It's no great mystery, we all know, money establishes the power, first and foremost, and the power lies in the hands of those who are in control of the money. Right? No argument there. This is lesson A-1 since time began, since someone put a stamp of a face on a piece of metal and said, there, that'll count for your day of work. If you move the money around more freely, if you are the mover, and you're the one with the power.

Oh, that's just jack shit, Quince said. No one has power over me. Look! And he stuck a finger into his nose, grinding out a nugget. He held it out for a moment, taunting, then popped it in his mouth and held it there and said through tight lips, Just try and stop me. He got a good laugh over that one.

No it isn't, you ignorant ass puss! Piston said, waving a hand, offended, back arched. You're not even listening.

Well then you tell us why it isn't jack shit, smart guy, and watch the name-calling.

It isn't jack shit, I'm telling you. And he tapped his temple with a finger. Tool of observation! That's what you're missing. The people with the power are the people with the money are the people who own everything and deal it out in little tiny piecemeal bits just to keep us from raiding the big table, to hold us off, you know, that's all minimum wage is, that's all welfare is, just a tossed down, gnawed on bone left-over to say back off you niggers, injuns, spicks, white trash shitheads and all you other scraggly little immigrant motherfuckers, just back off. Here's your scrap. And he threw down an invisible bone to the floor and said, See, there's your dinner!

And you think the money people have all the power?

Absolutely. Piston nodded and clamped his teeth on his cigarette. A child could see it.

And the people with the power have the money.

Dat's right. That's always been right. Well not right, but true. Just look where you are.

Well then, if you're going to take some of that power, how do you propose to move the money around? Seems like that's a freight train bigger than your muscles! And more laughter rippled through the smoke.

That's...that's the antitrust....what laws are supposed to do. That's what we elect these liberal motherfuckers for.

And do you see anything changing? T-Bear asked.

Nope. Because those liberal motherfuckers are just doing what everyone's doing, trying to survive. They're just throwing down a bigger bone is all. But you look behind their backs and you'll see they got a heap of gold in the cave they're holding onto. No secret. You can't scream justice cause nature ain't about justice. It's about survival. Dog eats dog. That's no secret.

Doesn't that tell you something?

It tells me those liberal motherfuckers want to keep a little too much for themselves!

Don't you see, T-Bear said, waving an arm as if he were trying to pull back the veil of smoke. It isn't the money. If it were the money alone, then you'd see them shifting away from it in a hurry, because that's too vulnerable. Thieves eventually find their way into the vault. Money's never been more than a symbol for the real thing, and the real power is more than the money. It's something much deeper than that!

Which is?

Ownership.

Right, ownership.

That's part of it, ownership and greed.

So what?

I'm saying you can't move any money around because that won't change anything. I'm saying it's a shell game. You're looking at the shells. The shells are always empty. T-Bear swept his hand forward and across in a cutting motion, deal done.

What the hell you mean? It would change everything. Why do you think they hold onto it so tightly?

The money is nothing. It's the perception that matters. You're the guy in the audience who thinks the magician is real. But it's all a trick. It's always been a trick. Making you believe it's real is the trick. Let me ask you something, T-Bear said. Let's just say you win the lottery.

Piston grinned and said, It could happen. It was as if he had a hold of something, and it lit up his eyes.

All right, smart guy, T-Bear continued. Let's say you win the lottery, say it's a big one, millions, billions...whatever ions. What are you going to do?

Me? Piston laughed and stood up and gyrated and said, You know I'm going to party party party.

There you go. T-Bear swept his hand out flat again, deal done.

What? I know what you're thinking. You're thinking I'm going to blow it all, that I'm going to be like those dumb bastards on TV who get all this money and blow it all and even make it worse and go into debt and can't pay their taxes and wind up in jail, blah blah blah.

Well...

Well, what? I'm not an idiot. I already see that. No one's tricking me! I already have a plan. I'd put some of it into savings. Just flat clean and simple stick a big chunk of it into savings. Don't even touch it. Pretend it's not even there. Even at....what, the little interest it makes, it makes something. And the more you put in the more it makes. I know that. I've got the big heap behind my back. And like they say, money makes money. So, I get money and I make sure it gets to work making more money. And I'll tell you what, after I take care of a few of my friends—that's right, I'll honor my friendships, and I won't step over all of you to go hang out with the other rich people with money. I know where I come from, see? And that's the mistake those other fools make. I'll take my friends on a cruise to the Bahamas or the Virgin Islands or...wherever ain't destroyed yet, someplace clean, yeah, and we'll hang out on a little island, just to enjoy it because you should get to enjoy it, right? You should get to party, swim, party. Come on! But then! 'Cause I'm no fool, I put some into savings, just to rest safely. And I hire one of those tough motherfucker investors, you know, the ones with the connections, like what's that bull one, you know, with the ring in its nose? Get someone who really knows the machinery of the system and how to do the work. Why do the work yourself if you can hire someone else to do it? Isn't that the whole reason for having money? A banker don't farm and grow his own food! A brain surgeon don't operate on his own head! So, yeah, I get the bull guy. What's he called?

Bullshit! Quince said, and the room erupted into laughter.

Very funny, very funny. No, but come on now, you know the one I mean. What's it called? He shook his hand like it hurt. Lynch something.

Yeah, they're going to lynch your savings. Laughter.

Lynch you for your money!

Yeah, Lynch something, whatever, you know what I mean? Piston looked around for an ally. He wanted to make this point clear to someone. This was very real, now, as if he already had the money in his hand. Whoever the powerhouse guys are on the inside, that's what I'm talking about. I'll find them. The money opens the doors. I get those guys and they just make me more money. And because they get a…a…percentage, they *want* to make money. That's how it works. They make me money, but they make themselves money at the same time too. They love it. Like hunting dogs. They love doing it cause it's the way they're wired. They're naturals. Ducks in water. They're made to make money. Maybe they don't have it to begin with, but they figure it out and work for the ones who have the money. And that's what I am now. So they make money for me and get some for themselves and make more money with it so I don't never have to work again, and I just take my friends on more cruises to the Bahamas and we party, party, party. He gyrated and pressed his fists together.

You don't work now!

I wanna go on that cruise! Take me along.

I'll take all ya'll along.

Piston probably end up seasick.

Get malaria.

Berry Berry.

Do they still have that?

Don't forget your shots, Piston.

Ah, he'll just drink enough to kill off any bug gets into his body.

Start a new strain.

Stronger, drunker mosquitoes.

Killer mosquitoes.

Coming up the coast of California with noses like Samurai swords!

What do you call those?

What?

Not noses.

Pro something. I went to high school.

Pro…pro-ba

Probation!

You fucking idiots. You're all just jealous, now, Piston said, 'cause I got the money. Better be nice to me now, you know. That's how it works.

But look what you just did, T-Bear said. Smart man says control the money and you have the power. You make the money move. The money that moved right into your lap, and you just turn it right back over to the ones who had it in the first place.

A money lap dance! Someone shouted.

Make it rain!

Give old Grant a kiss.

Hey, Piston, can I get a short-term loan?

You can see him, but you can't touch him.

You can only look.

Smart man has money move right into his home, T-Bear said, bringing both hands down in a funnel motion to his chest. All that money moving his way, and what does he do?

He buys a house!

We're going on a cruise!

Lifetime of cigarettes.

He dies of a heart attack!

Piston stopped and pointed a finger at the man. Don't you talk about me dying, now.

What does the smart man do? T-Bear asked, and now everyone wanted to hear it, like they knew he was about to put the last cut into Piston's already crumbling logic, because they all knew it just can't be, even if the fantasy is fun and making fun of Piston is fun. But Piston is never going to be rich. The eyes in the room focused now like a wolf-pack circling a coyote. They just wanted to hear T-Bear explain it. They wanted him to finish it off.

Smart man turns right around and gives it back! To the bank? To the ones on the inside? Smart man gets the money by buying that little ticket, and when the money comes to him he just moves it right back where it belongs, where it's always been. Because look at it, just look: he only thought he had it. Best shell and pea game ever, my man, and you're falling for it every day.

Ah, so what. They're used to money. They know how to handle it, so what? I'm still living large.

You're just the court jester.

Yeah, well, better the jester than the slave!

I don't see much difference, T-Bear said. The levity had deflated and now Piston was up and over getting into T-Bear's face, finger only inches from the other man's eyes.

Look, Indian, I don't see much call for you putting me down like that.

Hey, Piston, someone said, cool down!

T-Bear said nothing.

Piston stayed fixed in place. So what if I want to enjoy my life. So what if I want to share it with my friends? What's wrong with that? And so what if I flip the switch and make the ones who made me nothing work for me? Why do you have to cheapen it?

I'm not trying to cheapen it, T-Bear said. I'm telling you it wasn't worth anything to begin with. I'm telling you it's an illusion. Money won't buy you respect from the people who lived with it their whole lives. It won't buy you a world you can't already touch. It won't give you anything that won't exact something from you in return.

Are you saying it's better to be poor? Are you saying it's better to eat shitty food and sleep in shitty rat hole hotels like this one? Piston was so close to T-Bear's face that he looked like he might bite him.

I'm saying you'll just be in another kind of shitty hotel even with your money. Money's the trick. If money were the solution, don't you think smart and good and compassionate people would have devised a way to, as you say, move it around by now? Even if you move it, what it represents will still be hidden from you. And what is hidden will still be just another trick to keep you believing they're over you by making you believe you're under them. That's the illusion that keeps the rich rich and the poor poor.

Now you're talking nonsense. Money in your hand is real. The things it buys are real. Talk to me about illusions. Piston turned away shaking his head and someone handed him the jug and he drank a deep drink and held the bottle against his chest, but he continued to point his finger, saying, You mean for me to believe money doesn't matter. Well, you're the one living in an illusion, buddy, because I'll tell you something: money does matter. Money is the only thing that matters. Look at your people. They aren't where they are because money doesn't matter. And they sure as hell aren't building casinos because money doesn't matter. You try and eat. You try and find a place to sleep without money and see how far you go.

You talk as though I haven't lived in this world, T-Bear said. But all you're telling me is how many people are tricked by the same illusion. You're telling me the illusion is real.

Ah! You just twist it around, don't you, mister philosophical, but you're right here with the rest of us. Ain't that right? He shook his head and turned his finger back on himself like it was a gun. That's right. You're right here with us.

Then T-Bear smiled.

Hey Piston, someone shouted, keep that bottle moving.

After the party was over and everyone gone and all the smoke cleared and they were alone in their room, he pulled off his shirt and turned like a matador and sat down beside her on the bed and put his arm around her. They said nothing because there was nothing left to say with all that talk already heading on to the next city with roadies loading the last ahhs and umms into the equipment cases. He kissed her. She kissed him. A hummingbird hovered at the window, moving along a palm leaf with its long beak and blur of wings. It seemed to be looking at her. She felt a hand sliding over her belly. She closed her eyes in dissolving. They twisted through an array of divisible and collateral poses and just as slow in motion as her mind falling back into the bed like a hole in space open as though molded for their forms in particular and sinking into a web that kept them poised above a cauldron of rooms below and something ferrous bubbling even further down than that. And they made love in the heat of the evening, in the sounds of the city like an avant garde soundtrack, an abstract howl of ocean waves or crowd cheers rising from a stadium, rising and falling against the walls themselves trembling with a vicious living sheen. And in the same way she was aware of their mechanical actions she was taking in all the rooms and all the occupants in their shadow motion through that endless succession of walls and corridors, faces and voices, days and nights flickering like that broken bulb he held in his hand in a strobe of constant layered moments. And when at last they fell away from each other and his breathing became a measured slow hint of phlegm gurgle, even though it went against her en garde nature, she felt and allowed the light tendrils of an earthly luring resonance to wrap around her and set her adrift sliding down into a state of sleep as deep as she had ever known.

And she had this dream:

She is walking down a city street at dawn. Alone. Fog rides the air like another world wanting in. She feels eyes, feels watched, looks up and sees that hummingbird over her shoulder. People appear on the move like they know where they're going, yet some like her seem tentative as though trying to read street signs that aren't there, and others go around in circles or up against walls from which they bounce back only to go forward and hit again. One outline stands bent looking down and tapping an extended foot as if to determine whether or not the ground could hold all this human weight. But she is self-trained to disguise and assume the appearance of one in the know and scanning and acutely aware, keeping absolutely accurate track of the streets she walks and in what direction, a map burning into the mind. A motel with empty parking stalls, then a grocery store, a used car lot full of old cars no one will ever drive, billboards with layers of advertising showing through from the strips of images peeling off, a face beneath a plane and a skyscraper torn from a dreamy tropical beach. Remnants of a gone world. She passes an empty schoolyard and thinks it must be early in the morning or a holiday. Not a kid in sight. There is no sun visible, nothing to gauge direction. Her legs feel numb and she calculates sitting down somewhere, but she's afraid to cease moving, as though to stop would call attention to her, and these otherwise unconscious zombies would suddenly wake up and turn and descend on her like flies.

She is aware of her dreaming and in touch with herself outside the dream, of her own mind like an audience watching this consciousness trying to figure out the mystery of its own theater. She is not fully a part of this world. Isn't this how she usually dreams, with a tether to the waking world? But now something else is happening. When she draws back to feel herself, she's not sure anymore if the space she rises into is the real location of herself. She can't seem to detect it. It's as if something were sitting on her chest inhaling every breath she exhales. It seems perhaps this time she's gone a few layers deeper than before. But that could just be part of dream thinking. The ground seems real enough, but everything else around her, the gray trees like hooded figures, the demolished cars, the building fronts with vague, blue outlines behind them, everything shimmers with the gauzy thinness of the unreal. When she sees a woman standing on the steps of an old house in the middle of the block, something about her seems like a left over from another age, a holdout to the wave of progress, a developer's thorn, both woman and home, there between a condemned theater and a massage parlor. It's a dark, gothic multi-gabled house with a bower of bougainvillea over the porch so thick it makes a tunnel, and the woman there is like some strange earth gnome of prairie haze with arms gnarled as wisteria vines, holding a candle on a little green platter with a curved handle, the hand shaking with palsied rhythm so that the candle dances and the flame wavers. And with her other hand the old woman is vigorously waving with fingers curled into tiny feelers, come, come! She approaches, but the old woman does not stop motioning to her until she climbs the steps and stands one step below the old woman so that she and the woman are eye to eye, the old woman's hand still drawing her in, the eyes deep embedded in the putty of her face. She is an ancient relief of fleshy jowls, heavy lobed ears, white-gray cloud hair, and she is quite stooped though not very tall to begin with. She is a force of will, the hand waving the young girl in closer, close enough in fact for the old woman to reach out and touch her arm, which she does. The old woman wears brown gardener's pants splattered with paint and a white blouse covered by a brown wool sweater in which thorns and thistles and pieces of moss cling as though the woman had crawled out of the earth itself.

How old do you think I am? the old woman asks.

Not a day over thirty-nine.

The old woman smiles and for a moment it seems her eyes disappear.

I'm one hundred and twenty three, says the old woman, and she pats her chest with her hand as if to show the heart is still there. Yes I am. According to the records. I lived here long before they even had paved streets. Can you imagine that? There was a time when there were no roads. I saw them lay the cobbles for the first road. Yes I did. I saw all these buildings go up. She sticks out the candle to point at the ghostly neighborhood that surrounds her. More than one man come around with offers to buy my place, my land. I knew they wanted to tear it down, drive me away, but they never drove me out. They never bought me out. They never had enough money.

Why did you stay?

Where would I go anyway? I've got work to do here, and this is where it has to be done. This is the first place I came to when I came into my power. I was seventeen. I'd been all over the country before that. We came over from England. I've lived in every state, north and south, east and west. My father was a teacher, a composer, a mathematician, a traveling musician, a medicine man. Oh, we had parties. Every night a party. Paderewski gave me my first dollar. Yes she did. I babysat for Alma Gluck. Always music, every night. And people, people with talent and energy and charisma. Always a party. And the music. I loved the music most of all. Learned to play the piano myself. My father caught me with a sheet of ragtime, once, and when he saw that piece of sheet music he tore it to pieces in front of my face. He said no respectable girl plays that kind of music. That was his opinion, and he had other rules. And always moving from place to place. Never one place long enough that I could make a friend. I've never had a friend in this life. I got tired of it. I was tired of moving around, always moving. We got here and I just said, I'm not moving anymore. I'm not going to budge. My father said, fine. He gave me fifty cents, and that was the last time I saw him.

He never came to see you?

I never went to see him. Why should I? He left me. I was on my own after that. It was a terrible thing to do to a girl, leave her alone. But I was coming into my mystery then. I could feel it. But he was a good man. He really was. He died acting a gentleman. He was about to get on a streetcar but stepped down to allow two ladies to board before him. He was struck by another car going the other way, and that's what killed him. Not right off, though. He lingered for a few days, I'm told. And I'm told he was waiting for me to come to him. But I never did. The old woman's face shows nothing, no more emotion than a cliff rock blasted by wind. He passed on. His whole life was passing on. And he suffered more than most. His wife, my mother, was killed by a misfiled prescription, you know. The pharmacist read it wrong, poisoned her dead. Her best friend came out from England to help us, you know. It seemed like she was waiting to do that. I'm not a suspicious person, but the whole matter didn't sit right with me. Not that I think my father capable of a thing like that. But all I know is a story about it. I was young. Then this friend comes out from England, and she and my father get married right away. Like I said, something didn't sit right with me about that. I never took to her, but she got sick with the goiter. Sticking out of her neck. Awful thing. And it gave her the poppy eyes. She hanged herself. I found her when I came home one day after school, hanging in the foyer. That was it for my father, too. Something went out of him. Restless spirits, all of them.

How sad. That must have been hard on you, too.

Oh, yes, but you know I had to work, right away. A woman alone in those days had to work hard. I went to school, got a real estate license and then a nursing degree. I worked in a hospital. I delivered thirteen babies. But I've got to deliver one more, now, to end on a good number. And I got married too, had three children. My husband died, though, too soon. He drowned when we were on vacation out on the coast, Indian land. He was a strong swimmer, which is the strangest thing. He went out for a swim one evening and didn't come back. We searched. I was frantic. I remember an Indian boy riding a horse back and forth along the crest of the shore to try and see him. He was the one who spotted him because he was up high like that. They pulled him in, but he was drowned. After that I had to work even harder, you know? I worked the night shift at the hospital and got home in time to get my children off to school. Then I'd sleep.

Then I'd be up when they got home from school. That was the way it had to be. I should never have gotten married again after that, though. I married my second husband because I thought my children needed a father. I didn't want them going through life with others saying they had no father. But he turned out to be a drinker. I didn't know that at first. He came from a good family. They had a house out on the island and a boat. We went there in summer. But then he started to drink like he didn't want to be himself anymore. He used all my savings, the money from the insurance when my first husband died, and he opened up a produce warehouse. But he couldn't run it in his condition. And then there was the other matter, but I'm not going to talk about that. He just drank up all my money. A cruelness showed itself, and the children shouldn't have that and the way he treated them. I divorced him. Nobody divorced in those days. But living with him was worse than getting divorced. He was not a good man with my children. So I raised them on my own, and I told them, because you don't have a father you have to be even better than other kids because that's what everyone will say about you if you aren't— ah well, they'll say, it's to be expected, and of course they're no good, they don't have a father. But they turned out all right.

That's sad.

Now don't you go feeling sorry for me. I didn't tell you all that to get your pity. I'm long past that anyway. I see you scurrying around now all full of might and right and I'm just warning you, you see? That's the point after all. I'm giving you a warning, plain and simple. This story is yours now, part of you, now, and you can't forget it even if you try. I'm giving you a piece of my power, although I can see you have plenty of your own anyways. But sure enough and have no doubt, I'm giving you a warning.

About what?

About where you're going. About what it takes to get where you need to be. You're flipping coins, girl. I see where you're headed, and I'm just trying to help you stay clear of trouble.

What kind of trouble?

The same trouble I've seen. The same trouble I've had, some of which can't be helped, but if you think hard, look at things as they really are, there's a way you don't have to suffer so much. Your life is bound to come on it, of course, every life does. But you have to know what to do when it happens. It's a way of your mind more than anything. Doesn't matter so much where you are or what you're doing, although those things are important, too. And your story is going to fit into others, you know, so it's not just about you. But what matters most is how you think.

How am I supposed to think?

Simple and clear, like I'm telling you. No fooling around with what you want to be but what is. I mean you can make yourself into any character, but you're also nothing but what you are and you got to keep an eye on that too. Most people can't do that. They look at things how they want them to be instead of how they are, then they get all fussed up when things end up ways they don't want. It's like people expect miracles when they should just step aside from trouble plain in front of their faces. That's where your strength lies. You see it clear and don't fool yourself. You have a good detector, use it. That's what I'm trying to tell you. And you take it with you. It's what you already have, but I'm also giving you something because you'll remember this. That's the way a story works. You understand what I'm saying? And you'll have to tell your own, too. But right now, I'm giving you mine. It's got fire in it. You need some fire. You got plenty of the other, but you need more fire. You will need it someday, that's plain to see. It's not so strange. Don't think too much about it. A woman gave it to me just like I'm giving it to you. It's something you should have been taught long ago and weren't. You should have had that training, but you didn't get it. It's not your fault. Changes aren't just these roads and buildings. There's other things, things that people think are lost, but they're never lost. They just come to us in different ways. It will come to you as well to pass this on to another one day. You'll know when that time comes. It won't be anything you plan. It will be something you carry with you always, and you have always had it though you didn't know you had it. I am just here to show it to you and give you a piece of mine. Now you can go. You can tell people about the strange old woman you met and her sad story, but that won't be it. And the story is not so sad as you think, if you think about it. You can laugh about me or disbelieve me, but that won't be it, either. Now you go on. You've got to look like you're going somewhere. I've done my job now. Now I got fourteen, and that's all I need. I can end on a good number, like I said. So, you go on, now. Don't let those shadows catch you with your mouth open.

And the woman waves her back down the steps in a reversal of the motion she used to draw her onto the porch in the first place, and just as it was impossible to resist that summoning she is now unable to resist the will that sends her away, glancing back once to see the old woman waving at her insistently, ripples in the air visibly flowing out from her hands until she finally turns and ducks back into her bower of blood-red vines that tremble like living arms into a tunnel that leads for all she knows down to the core of the earth.

She awoke to the sound of rain. It came in through the window cool and wet like a blessing, like forgiveness, and she reached out her hand and felt it on her palm and tasted it and lay there listening to it long into the night, its sound like waves rolling across the rooftops and over the bland faces of the buildings and over the window ledges, blending with the waves of cars passing in the street below, their tires hissing, the sound of it hypnotic, rhythmic, full of melody and little voices, like all the languages of the world in a chorus of pure breathing and occasional distant thunder, like the edge of the world in crumble, a great river coming down and swallowing up the streets and the buildings and the sad wandering people hitting up against lampposts and walls.

ANIMAL SPIRITS

tuart's mother did not believe him. She made her way over to their house after she was finally convinced by the police that her son was dead, and she wanted to know exactly what happened. Gabriel told her. She narrowed her eyes and pointed a finger at him and said, You knew he was a frail boy. You knew. Why did you let this happen? You're to blame. You know that, don't you? You let this happen. You let things go too far. You should have been watching out for him!

I told him not to go, Gabriel said.

I'm so, so sorry, Gabriel's mother said, It's a horrible accident. She stood by him, but she didn't touch him, and he understood in some way she was allowing the woman to blame him, even though she was also defending him. The woman was shaking with rage. But what could she do? Without another word, she went past him and through the door and left. But he still felt her eyes burning him where he stood.

I didn't want—he began, but confused thought choked his mind.

I know, his mother said, her hand light on his shoulder.

He woke up early, before light. He dressed in the dark and carried his backpack down to the kitchen and dropped it on the floor by the screen door. His father had already made bacon and eggs and toast and coffee. Gabriel sat down and rubbed his eyes and waited. His father put a plate before him and he ate.

Better than going to school, don't you think? his father said. He stood by the counter eating from a plate of his own, smiling. He rarely sat at tables.

Definitely.

Let's hope we get a good haul this year.

After his father finished eating and put his plate in the sink, he said, Well, you about ready to go?

Sure.

They went down to the truck, and Gabriel pushed his pack into the space behind the seat and climbed up into the cab. His father slid in and closed the door and started the engine and turned on the lights. Ahead, the trees were a tunnel of dark trunks and boughs illuminated by the headlights. They moved down the gravel driveway and out onto the road.

His father went into a silence of his own, and they drove north in the dark then out onto the highway that was nothing but clear lanes white lines and blue reflectors at this hour. Then they pulled off onto an access road that went down into town. The streetlights were fixed and blinking yellow. The streets were empty. It was like an end of the world movie, still and heavy. Then they drove up to the ferry terminal, paid the cashier in the booth and went onto the ferry.

They stayed in the truck cab for the crossing with its smell of earth and mink oiled boots and rifle iron. Gabriel's father opened a window and lit a cigarette and smoked and blew the smoke out the window and leaned back in the seat and turned on the radio. He fiddled with the dial across talk and static and came to a Hank Williams song and let it sit. The ferry horn sounded three times and the boat pulled out into the sound and rocked softly on its way. Out there was the blackness of the water, the far faint lights of homes on islands. What was it like to live on an island? It seemed like a perfect dream and at the same time a little sad. He didn't want his life the way it was, now that he was a bad kid. On an island he would be alone.

Daylight was coming on, glowing up behind the eastern mountains across the sound as they drove off the ferry and onto a two-lane highway heading toward the peninsula. Then they were back driving through the darkness with nothing but the forest eyes. They went through a mill town with its rot-smell and sandstone buildings blasted by wind and sea wave spray and then back into the corridor of trees fluttering in the car lights and Sasquatches watching from the forest deep. The road was becoming as they drove because you've got to believe a road to drive on, just as in reality they were asleep in their beds, asleep in their lives and would wake up wondering about these scenes that fast fade as they swim into that other world becoming people going to sleep and waking up in other worlds and on and on maybe forever and this is what he kept thinking as they drove through the dark.

Emerging at last they entered a clearing, and his father drove onto a gravel road and out into a field of clearcut where the stumps of trees stood flat-topped and gray and other trees lay like dead soldiers. The truck came to a stop, and his father stubbed out a cigarette and opened the door and stepped out and stretched and scanned the field. Gabriel got down and walked a few feet out in front of the truck and gazed over the wasted forest edge. Every tree was cut down all the way up to the ridgeline before the forest started again. A few trees lay on the ground, and some saplings twigged their way up through the ground cover. Robins jumped and darted and flew stump to stump, and they seemed weirdly exposed. Tendrils of mist rose from the ground. The air was raw, and as Gabriel stood before the ticking engine of the truck he had a dizzy feeling he had seen this before.

Well, his father said, better get started. He took the chainsaw out of the back of the truck and hiked out over the roughed-up terrain. Gabriel followed, climbing over dead trees. The ground was a loamy tangle and he had to choose his footing carefully. His father took long strides, lifting his feet high, and would occasionally stop and inspect a tree, pull at it then move on until he finally found the one he wanted. He punched the choke on the chainsaw and was just about to pull the cord when he turned and said, I want you to stand back while I'm cutting. When I'm done you can help me load the truck. Then he yanked the cord and the chainsaw screamed and he started carving into a fallen tree.

Gabriel climbed up onto a stump and watched as his father cut slice by slice, bucking and lifting the log and propping it so he could cut it all the way through, tugging back and laying down the blade again and cutting length by length as the chips grew around his feet. It was like their basement full of sawdust and the smell of wood and wood oils and stains and varnishes and machines for cutting wood and for shaping wood, and here he was now his father the crafter with his arms deep into wood.

It didn't take long to cut the trunk down into moveable sections. All right, his father said, turning to Gabriel and brushing the sawdust from his chest. Give me a hand here. Gabriel jumped down. He could only take a chunk at a time, while his father's armloads seemed heaped high. But he worked steadily and didn't complain. His arms soon felt hot and tired and ached and his back felt tight-strained, but he kept on working and said nothing as his father worked on and said nothing.

After they finished loading the wood, his father lit another cigarette and stomped around in search of another fallen tree. When he found one to his liking, he yanked at it, getting it into a position ready for cutting and pulled the cord on the chainsaw and set the blade in while a cigarette bobbed between his teeth and his eyes squinted and sawdust boiled up over his hands. They loaded more sections onto the truck then his father sought another tree, and after he had sliced up that one they had a full load.

We're done, his father said. He stood smoking another cigarette, looking out over the clearcut. Sweat was flowing down his face, and he wiped it with his sleeve. Gabriel stood beside him, leaning back against the fender of the truck. The sun was breaking through the clouds and warming the ground. The stumps steamed like hot bodies. Chipmunks appeared from the tangle and jumped across fallen logs and stumps, rising up and looking around with forepaws dangling against their bellies.

Well, his father said, is that enough work for ya?

Yeah, Gabriel said, and he blew a long breath.

What do you say we go get a cheeseburger?

Sounds good to me.

Let's go.

They climbed into the truck and backed up onto the service road.

The truck moved heavy with its load, straining in a new way as they bounced on through the washouts and potholes of the uneven ground to the main highway.

They ate lunch in a roadside diner with trucks and semis pulled up in the dirt lot and men in plaid shirts and John Deere caps who smoked and drank endless cups of coffee and talked of bad brakes and mushy suspensions and burn-offs and logging rights and the collapsing government. And then they were back on the road, driving through the marching trees again. The clouds burned off and sunlight came piercing through. The radio jumped around slipping from its stations, so his father switched it off. They opened the windows and the cabin filled with the sweet pine smell of the forest. And slowly, through glades and turns and far from any town the road descended and the trees began to change to alder and maple and madrona, thinning out as the road dropped and rose and dropped again winding out towards the coast. Smell it? his father said.

What?

The sea.

It emerged and retreated like a shy living thing, and Gabriel was awake and alert, search-gazing hard through the trees. Was that a silver flash of wave? Was that the glitter of light on the surface? Was that blue of it shining in the distance? And then they came to a turnoff and drove bumping and jolting to the road's end at a trail head marked by a row of bleached driftwood. His father switched off the engine. Here we are, he said.

They climbed out and unloaded the gear. Gabriel put on his pack, and his father pulled down the straps so that it was cinched tightly around his shoulders and waist and pressed close against his back. Then his father put on his own pack and tugged the straps down tight and stuck his arms out and lifted them and worked his shoulders and then said, Well, then…let's go.

His father set off up the trail and into the woods, and Gabriel followed, leaning forward, striking for a balance that would put the weight of the pack right in the middle. Sometimes he felt it pulling him back and so he leaned forward. Then he felt it pushing him forward so that his steps were a kind of catch-up. And so he weaved along the trail, toe-stumping roots and rocks when he didn't pay attention to his footing. Gradually, he found the right stride, hooking his thumbs under the shoulder straps and keeping his eyes on the path. His father strode ahead and out of sight. Occasionally Gabriel caught glimpses of him through the trees or when the trail curved back on itself, and from time to time his father would call out, You all right back there?

I'm all right. Are you all right? And he would hear his father laugh. And that became their call and response for hiking, his father calling back, Are you all right back there? And Gabriel answering, I'm all right, you all right?

After a while the straps felt like they were cutting into Gabriel's shoulders, and his arms began to tingle, a feeling that went to the bone. But he said nothing and kept up the call and response with his father. He was hot, thirsty, mouth dry from hard breathing. But he pushed to follow and keep up. The trail descended switch-backing down the hillside. Sunlight came through in dusty rays. The forest floor was thick with moss-covered logs and thistles and nettles and ferns. Fat banana slugs stretched across the trail, and Gabriel stepped around them while keeping up his stride. And then he found a rhythm that allowed him to move with a steady grace, focused on the path and his footing even as he sought in quick glances for a glimpse of the sea.

And at last he saw it. A high tone flash. Then it was gone. He listened and heard a whisper from the distance. Then he saw it again, glittering through the trees. He was certain of it. And the whispering returned.

His father called back, You all right back there?

Gabriel answered, I'm all right, you all right?

Then he saw it full through the opening in the trees huge and blue with a white ragged surf edge and a hard dark line far far out and then sky. He came down to where the path leveled out and saw his father standing there, hands on his hips, smiling, not even breathing hard. How you holding up? his father asked.

Good.

Thirsty?

Yeah.

His father grabbed the stays of his pack and turned him around and tugged on a pouch and pulled out a water bottle and handed it to him. Then he reached back to a side pouch on his own pack and pulled out a water bottle and drank and poured some of the water over his face and shook his head and said, Ahhhh. Not much farther, now.

Okay.

You done with that? his father said, pointing at Gabriel's bottle with the tip of his own.

Yeah.

His father took the bottle and slipped it back into Gabriel's pack, then put his own water bottle back into the side pouch and said, Last leg. Let's go.

They followed the trail through swampy glades and crisscrossing creaks, descending gradually. The ocean was coming to them, moving under and into the land as the trees seemed to stand back for it. Seagulls rose crying over the treetops as if saying this way this way. Then the trail dipped down and the sea was gone from view. But when the trail rose again the sea was there before them, and Gabriel felt the rush of it in the surge of wind and the salt smell and taste, the water rolling huge and cobra-bent, coiling and suspended briefly then crashing tumbling and roiling under churning white foam as it stretched out at last thin and green and glassy as the seagulls with their wings in perfect hard arcs rode the breeze over the breaking waves. Gabriel stood rapt before the enormity of it like this unbound by islands and the sound and fully open all water, his first vision of the true sea.

They set up a camp in the grass behind a line of tangled driftwood where the last few trees blocked some of the wind and where a little creek flowed down and fanned out shimmering onto the beach. His father pitched the tent and built a fire ring while Gabriel gathered firewood. They shook out the sleeping bags and tucked the packs into the foot of the tent, and his father hung a bag from a tree limb to keep their food safe from bears and other ground critters. Then he spread a blanket out before the opening of the tent and the campsite was set.

Gabriel walked balancing along the driftwood logs with his arms out and then jumped into the sand. He looked out at the ocean, the curve of the horizon. Not one ship out there, only the sea. Then he went down where water came sliding fast, the wet sand shimmering like polished stone. The sun was low and warm, and the wind wild off the sea was full of intensity. Gabriel could lean into it and feel his body suspended as if a hand were pushing him back. He sailed sand dollars and they came alive and hawks flew scanning overhead. He knelt down near a tide pool and overturned a rock and saw little black-shelled crabs scattering. He picked one up and it dug its stony limb-points into his fingers. He looked into the orbit of its white-tipped, milky eye. What do you see, my little friend? He put it back and replaced the rock and continued down the shore.

And as he walked on he saw towers of rocky chunks of land that looked like they were marching in slow motion out to sea with a few scrag pines embedded up top and hanging on with exposed roots like arms gripping hard to the earth. He wandered among them feeling like a little crab among giants. He picked up a heavy stick and dragged it through the wet sand, leaving a long unbroken scroll of meaningless script. Then he wrote out his name in cursive letters along with stars and river waves and mountain tops like a map of everything he saw and at last a giant X to mark his spot. Then he threw the stick into the waves and watched it plunge and rise and drift in the currents, seeming to try for return.

He turned and headed back to camp, now facing into the wind and blowing sand that came at him stinging with speed. He put a hand up to protect his eyes. From a cliff of sandstone grooved by wind grinning faces gazed at him. The forest up the hill was dense. He looked but couldn't see where the trail came out. And then he saw something lift off, something too big to be a gull or even a hawk, moving slow in power soar, using the wind with a kind of liberty as it circled skyward and on, and as that eagle rose and cruised across the tree line and higher, Gabriel jumped and somehow went after it in a moment of breath and buoyancy as he flew by will alone yet with the air that carried him held deep in his chest.

When he returned to the camp, he dropped down onto the blanket. His father had a campfire going hot with a blackened pot nestled on a flat rock with beans bubbling away inside. He tossed in a couple of hotdogs and they sank and it all smelled good. He cut up some bread and cheese and apples and laid out a fine little meal on paper plates and handed one to Gabriel. The food was steaming hot. Gabriel blew on each forkful as he ate.

Not bad for a camp meal, eh? his father said. My grandfather used to cook bacon on a piece of wood, made it smokey, and oh that tasted good.

Grandpa with the spider?

That's right. You remember him? His name was Thomas High Bear, too, just like me, just like you. He wasn't the first High Bear, though.

What do you mean first?

Story I heard is our people used to live on the edges, hill people, river people. That side of the family sort of wandered around, never voted, never paid taxes, never went to school. They got the name out there, or were given, acquired you might say. The Crow, I might have heard, at least that's what my father told me, I think. Maybe Crow. I'm not sure.

Crow?

You never heard about that?

No.

The Crow...people.

Where?

I don't know. But anyway, one day, my grandfather went into a town, became another person and disappeared into a new life.

Wow.

Funny story, huh?

Yeah.

And then my father was born and he went to school and worked his way up as they say.

So...how did die?

My father?

Yeah.

He drowned, right here in the ocean just a little north of here. He and my mother were out here on vacation, and he went in for one last evening swim and drowned, caught in a rip tide. Some of the folks up there searched for his body using their fishing boats. He was always a strong swimmer, a powerful man. A boy riding a horse along the top of the shoreline spotted him, spotted the body. He went out with a lot of secrets.

And how did great grandfather die?

He died an old man. Lived out his life near Lake Chelan, ran a motel out there. We visited a few times, but I rarely saw him. He never much talked about his past to me or anyone else I know. I asked my mother about him some, but she just said he was a hardworking man, a good man.

How did they meet?

My parents?

Yeah.

In school. They were sweethearts in school. Ask grandma about it sometime. She likes to tell that story.

So how come you and mom call me Gabriel?

That's your middle name.

Yeah, but how come I don't go by my first name?

So we won't get confused when she calls us to dinner. Now, finish up there.

And his father tossed his empty plate into the fire where it sputtered and steamed and then burst into a quick flame burning from the center then gone. Gabriel ate the rest of his food and tossed his plate into the fire.

His father lit a cigarette and leaned back against a log and smoked with one hand behind his head. Gabriel lay flat on his back looking up at the stars as if he had never seen them before. Wow, he said, the stars are really bright out here, and so many.

Yeah, the city lights don't obscure it here. See that white streak? His father pointed with his cigarette.

Yeah.

That's the Milky Way.

What's that?

That's our galaxy. It's like our galaxy is a spinning octopus, and what we're seeing there is one of the arms of that octopus. Our planet is on another arm, but we can't see it because we're on it. And see that big collection of stars there, with the square and the part curving back?

I think so.

That's the Big Dipper.

The Big Dipper, Gabriel said, and then he saw something flare out in a quick and silent streak. What was that? he said.

A shooting star. Actually, they're not stars. They're bits of matter hitting the earth's atmosphere. Maybe little asteroids, comets, disintegrating satellites. Space garbage.

Wow.

We'll probably see more before the night's through. That's Orion there, his father said, running his hand back and forth over a spot of sky. You can tell by the three stars of his belt. And that's the little dipper, the little bear.

That sure is a high bear, Gabriel said.

His father laughed. Great grandfather riding high. Looks like he's smiling.

He is laughing.

At what.

You and me.

Why?

Cause we're looking at him.

All right.

It seemed to Gabriel that in some way out here his father was different, lighter. Before they'd left, Gabriel thought the purpose of the trip had something to do with Stuart and that somewhere along the way he was going to be lectured, but so far his father said nothing about it. They lay there a long time with the stars all around them. After a while his father rose and went out beyond the fire light, and Gabriel waited and listened and wondered. Then his father came back and tossed his cigarette into the fire and said, Well, I'm turning in. And he yawned and stretched and climbed into the tent. Gabriel listened to the rustling as his father slipped into his sleeping bag. Then Gabriel rose and went out to the creek and dipped his hands in and brought the cold water to his face and listened to the snapping of the fire and to the waves coming in on the beach below. Did he hear something else? Did he see something above? Another flash in the sky? Then he went back and climbed into the tent and lay down there in his sleeping bag beside his father, hearing the sounds of fire and sea and his father beside him breathing in the dark.

He stood before it, naked but for the cross on the little black cord around his neck. The sun was behind him, coming up over the trees. He stepped in and felt the first touch of it on his feet, a cold bite. He went forward until he stood with the water up to his knees, surging forward then surging back with the seemingly solid ground beneath him dropping away in circles where his feet were planted. He went farther, and the incoming water hit against his chest with its cold body-wracking force. Then he dove in.

The waves came in and he dove under them and felt them roll across his back, felt the fast sweep and lunge and weight of all that water and then a brief suspension where nothing seemed to move at all. Then he rose to the surface and sky above and horizon line and the diminishing curve of the shore. He swam beyond the breaking waves into the outer swells and felt his body rise and fall with the ocean. He swam parallel to the shore and outward too feeling a new kind of fear and freedom as he pushed forward and at the same time felt nudged and propelled in a thousand ways he couldn't control. He felt good and strong and dove down and swam in that green-hued and spiraling world. Then he rose and caught an incoming wave and rode it as it surged and gathered like a fist and rushed forward. He turned back and lunged out to catch another wave and rode it for a short distance before it left him. He went wave after wave and had a string of good rides, hitting just as the waves pulled into their full force, riding to shore and gliding into the rippling shallows.

Then there was a lull during which he floated and waited and watched as the swells came in, and he tried to gauge which ones would rise and carry him. He caught a few too early and swam hard to stay in, but they rolled right past him. He caught a few more, finding that magic spot not too high up and behind the force of the wave nor too far forward where he'd get hammered by the break. Then he found himself trying for one too late. It was already breaking, and he was caught up in its explosion and punched downward. He couldn't control himself and was thrown and dashed by the churning water. He rose to his feet in the foaming, broken wave and coughed and shook his head and leaned onto his knees. Then he dove back in and swam under the next three waves to a deeper place to tread water and wait and choose the next perfect wave.

He rode some, lost some, diving under some that seemed huge

and frightening. In the lulls he swam back and forth or dropped down to a pinging depth by letting the air out of his lungs, and when his feet struck bottom he bent his knees and pushed back surface-ward to break gasping into the air. Then he came up inside another wave that was just starting to break. He saw it only for a moment and barely had time to take a breath. It pounded down and sent him swirling under. When he rose, he was facing another wave and could only gasp once before he was thrown back under again. Then the waves had him in some terrible grip. He came to the surface only to see another wave in full crest, drawn back, as if gathering from its own collapse the force and energy for its next rise and fall. And Gabriel was inside it, swept forward and carried with it and under it, rolling completely lost. By luck alone he broke through for air before another wave came down on him and drew him under, and for a long heart-throbbing and chest-aching moment he couldn't tell how to get back and there were no rays of light to guide him to the surface.

There was a strange suspended moment with no idea of surface or depth, only the dark between wave-breaks stillness. His mind became a point, and the thought struck him that he was drowning the way his grandfather drowned, in the same place in the same waters—and it was as if that thought brought grandfather near, inside his mind, seeing this all over again in the body of his grandson and saying in a silent way, No. Gabriel swam as hard as he could in the only direction he could, wave after wave breaking upon him and taking him under, erasing the world. But he kept swimming, going forward, taking whatever breaths he could steal in the intervals of wave-crash, until he reached the shore and crawled out of the grip of the sea.

He collapsed dissolving into the sand, breathing hard but his mind deep down completely at ease. He felt nothing. Then he passed out.

When he woke, his body was shaking and tingling. He didn't know if he could stand. Where was his father? The salt crystallized on his skin. He rose to his feet and stood on trembling newborn legs. He looked down at his body and saw no injuries. He was amazed. He wanted to call out to someone and say, Did you see that? He laughed and shook his head and looked out at the sea now calm and beautiful. He lifted his hands and looked at them, he lifted his feet. I'm all right, he said. He placed his hands on his chest and took a deep loving breath and then realized that his cross was gone.

He put on his clothes and hiked back up the empty beach. An eagle swept along the upper edge of the tree line, and Gabriel raised his head and let out a sharp and piercing sound unlike anything he'd ever heard come from his own throat before. He leaped over the fallen driftwood and called every branch and every stone and every swirl of sand and swale of grass by new names. He followed the creek back into camp where his father was packing up the tent, a cigarette dangling from his lips. He said nothing to his father about the waves.

He helped collect up the last of their things and set his own pack against a log and slipped it onto his back by himself. He stood up, pulled the straps tight and said, I'm ready.

Well just give me a minute, there, cowboy. His father took a few last drags on his cigarette, then tossed it into the fire pit and kicked some dirt over it. He scanned the site and the sea one more time, then lifted his pack onto his back and cinched it and said, All right, then. Lead the way.

Gabriel leaned forward into the slope of the hill and used the weight of the pack to propel him. He concentrated on each heavy step, but he felt clear and crisp and strong. When he reached the first sharp switch-back he turned and took one last look at the sea glittering hard and blue through the trees and the waves singing with its infinite voices and then turned and hiked on, and gradually he couldn't distinguish the sound of sea waves from the sound of wind coming through the trees or at last from the sound of his own breathing.

Gabriel kept the lead the entire way and pulled his water bottle from the side pocket to drink only once at the same spot where they'd stopped before to drink on the hike in. And he called back, You all right back there?

I'm all right, his father said, You all right?

When they reached the car, Gabriel unhooked his pack and dropped it and stood breathing hard as his father came up after him.

Then they loaded their packs into the truck and climbed in. Crickets were clicking loud in the pine needles.

Well then, his father said. You ready to head home?

Yeah.

His father started the truck and pulled back around and headed out onto the road with the sun shining through the tree branches with a hypnotic fluttering of light.

A MEAN REVERSION

t was no surprise that when Jones appeared at work the next day he had no memory of missing the meeting, no memory in fact that there had been any meeting at all. The previous day retracted into the blur and baleen and inky bloom of dark undersea no thought could penetrate, and so as he ambled into the office it was again no surprise that because he had missed the meeting, he was called into George's office.

George was a thin to gauntness steel-haired company patrician with the cartilaginous features of one who sticks to business and off-market supplements, who knows how to keep a business functioning with precision and profit and a cool battleship commander's circumspection. His skin was pinkish and his eyes the palest of gray, but there was an intensity and acuteness about him that suggested nothing passed his scrutiny, no fraction miscalculated, no hair untouched, no pin out of place. And his office was a chamber of perfection with dustless and uncluttered desk, new black leather chairs, and a ceiling fan regulating the temperature to the precise degree for signing anything. Jones, he said, even though he and Jones were the same age and the same relative rank in the company but because of the office culture everyone called Jones Jones, We need to talk.

And Jones knew exactly what was coming. As if a plug were pulled from his navel, he let go a long stream of breath and dropped into one of the leather chairs facing George's desk and offered himself up for reprobation or worse.

I know, he said, while in fact he didn't know exactly what it was all about. Dejection in this environment was becoming a habit.

Jones, George said, sitting down on the front corner of his desk and crossing his hands on his lap. I'm not going to play some kind of heavy role with you here, but I'm going to tell you the truth.

Just as well. Jones felt that his hangover was now a dull blessing. He moved somewhere inside himself like a boxfish, insulated.

We're losing money, Jones. You know that, don't you?

In the market?

No, he said, turning his head slightly, squinting just perceptibly as if that were going to give a clue. How many clients do you have, Jones?

Jones pushed himself up in the chair. Mine are some of our biggest accounts.

How many?

Dozens or more, last time I counted.

George leveled his gaze at him. Two, Jones. You have two accounts. All your other clients have left the firm.

There was no retreat. That's ridiculous, Jones said. Why, I had three or four meetings scheduled just…and the other day, Mrs…

Gone. Whoever you're talking about. Probably gone. They've all pulled out. They all did. And they didn't go with other representatives here, either. And we're a team, Jones, all of us together from the newest to the most senior advisor. A team. So, I suppose the clients who left felt that it would have been some kind of insult to you to work with anyone else, which shows that they liked you that much. And for good reason, Jones. You're a good man. None of them named you, specifically, as the reason for their leaving, but come on, Jones, let's be honest; your drinking has gotten out of hand.

My drinking? Well, sure, I drink. So do a lot of the agents in the firm. It's part of the culture, part of the process, the panache, the dance with the client…

Well, it looks like you've been left on the floor by yourself. He raised his eyebrows as a coup d'etat, the final stab, then slid down to a lower depth of sincerity, opening his hands as though offering some kind of emolument. Now I don't mean to sound…judgmental or disrespectful, Jones. I like you. We've been friends for years. Your father gave me my first job. But I'm telling you, we're losing money.

That's preposterous! With all of the other agents?

We have to restructure. At this rate, we will be seriously in trouble and very soon. We aren't even making our overhead for office space and salaries right now. Do you know that?

But what about…? He didn't even want to say his name. Or…

Yes?

Jones rubbed his neck, looking down. Sunlight, miraculous sunlight, was coming through the window, inserting a square of light on the floor like an escape hatch he could simply step forward and drop through, and the temptation was very great at this moment, with George's eyes drilling him with white-hot intensity. It was mind-numbing. Mind-blinding. Why, why…all of them? All of my clients? How can that be? Not all of them, surely.

All of them, Jones. Where have you been? You haven't been to any of the meetings in weeks. When was the last time you actually met with a client? Really?

I thought…I thought, but wait!

Jones, you've got to get it together. Do you understand? We can't keep working like this, the firm can't stay like it is if you don't get some help, really, and soon. And not just for your job, Jones. You know? Do you understand?

What do you mean?

I mean your health.

I'm perfectly healthy! I'm fine! I'm fit! Strong as a bull!

Jones, I'm speaking to you as a friend.

Now wait a minute you little piranha… Jones rose from his chair, but he could not sustain the advance, saw no point in it as he looked down at the little mechanical man sitting there in his girlish pose, his mouth like a salt sucker with just the slightest hint of a grin. This was all theater. There was no question about it. Theater of the absurd! But he also knew that this was not George's way. George was not a bad man and had no real incentive to shame or even condemn Jones. In one province of his mind he knew what this was all about, the real truth of the matter, that the firm had to make money, and as long as the money was coming in, they were all friends and happy colleagues. Full steam ahead! Beyond that, there was nothing else that connected George and Jones, really, no other basis for their relationship other than a nostalgic connection to Jones's father, a connection which by now was not much more than semblance, eroded as it was by time and indifference.

Sorry about that, Jones said.

Jones, George said, what can I say? I'm not trying to hurt you. I'm just telling you what I see, and I see the best broker I ever knew destroying himself. We've been together for a lot of years, and in all that time I've been mostly in awe of you. Did you know that? No one hooks the clients like you do. No one keeps clients longer than you do. No one has ever had more clients than you. You're the Don Juan of brokers. But something happened. Somewhere along the way... what? You tell me, Jones, what? Because all I can see is the drinking. You're slipping badly, Jones, and, frankly, I'm scared for you.

Pinned and wriggling on the wall, Jones held his hands before him, two shaking tendrils not quite part of him, not fully under his command. He thrust them into his pockets. I...he began, but what was there to say?...I...I'm sorry. He turned.

Now, Jones. Don't just–

No, no. You're right, Jones said, retreating from the box of light on the floor, the smooth carpet, the angular windows, the high ceiling with its fan spinning like an executioner blade.

By eleven Jones was out the door and standing on the fire escape lighting a cigarette and taking in the fog horns, train whistles and seagull cries. The stairs and window ledges were covered with pigeon shit, and pigeons huddled in the window casing under disintegrated wire mesh. Old cigarette butts were everywhere, most of them his. And through his fingers the smoke went in and down and gave its mild narcotic nudge. A slight new glow to the dying arcade. A percolating cloud was mid-blossom and spreading like a bruise around a navel of sunlight over the city towers. He opened the door and looked inside and down the hallway with its telescoping fluorescent sheen. No one was there. He went down the fire escape stairs.

On the street of visors and heat-shield awnings and edge predators, he stepped around the pit holes and vent steam among people on the move, the sidewalks crowded with their energy. He put on a pair of dark glasses and felt comfortably invisible.

One drink.

He slid into McCormick's and took his usual place at the bar. The smooth dark wood gleamed like a holy altar. Two day drinkers were sitting a few seats down, and a few more sat in the booths. One couple eye-locked and whispery had the look of an illicit rendezvous. The bartender was familiar but nameless and popped up like a magpie to greet him, her hair pulled back so tight her skin was screaming. He focused on her avian nose and the two black stones in the eggshell face. What can I get for you, she asked. Her words shot out in quick chirps.

Johnny Walker Black on the rocks, he said. And she was already turning, already in the process of making it before he realized what he had said, responding automatically, and that he had not ordered food and would not order food and would order another drink as soon as the first one was done and would force himself not to finish it too quickly thinking also that he should have ordered a double.

Maybe you're a blue jay, he thought or said, as she placed the drink before him with her fingers thin as talons. The ice settled. The liquid relaxed from its dance in radiant waves as he put it to his lips, the purest libation, so cold and the scent of the alcohol rising to his nose before he even tasted it, tasting it in fact before he tasted it, then actually tasting it, cool smokey and warm, and at last the bright burn to the core of being. Ah, to be human again. Though not just human. Better than human. Superhuman. Full of the true, the beautiful, the blushful Hippocrene!

By the second drink, his soul reclaimed its seat of authority with interest and clarity, and it struck him that even his body had begun to find its edges again, its golden line, yes that's it, the form has been obscured by too much tension or lack of the correct tension, and this, this is the defining fire, all energies properly distributed throughout the limbs, the blood moving at its proper pace, chambers of the heart diastolically filling and systolically working and sending blood on its way. He could feel it happening, and it pleased him. If only he could sell this smile. And he said, aloud, The machine finds its magic again! He didn't really think anyone was paying any attention to him, but the two people at the end of the bar looked over for a moment, and so he continued, lifting his glass: To the heart, he said, and of course the soul!

A drink. Another drink. What lovely wood. Mahogany. Molten grain and depths like ocean layers going down, the wood is like a map of time and mind, down, down through the black burn of epochs, townships and the treaties, past the huts on the shores and the smoking fish, past Shem and Shaun, Adam and Eve and swerve of shore and time and river, river running down and around…

Can I get you something else? the bartender asked.

Yes, please. Another. And he held up his empty glass and rattled the ice. While she fixed him another drink, he followed the idea further: the heart expands to take in blood, and this action is called diastole. This is also, in linguistics or poetics rather, the lengthening of a syllable for poetic effect, as in suppose a line like: And there the king is but as a beggar, although the elimination of the word 'as' would be more concise. It must be added to make the line align to a correct number of syllables, but there you are again, back in the numbers, the golden mean, the line aligning with…ha, I suppose therein is the eternal example, the hidden gem as it were. There must be a name for that specifically and not just the umbrella of the broader poetics. And no neologism, although we're not opposed to those. Where would we be without invention? But back to the original line: isn't it much more interesting to say, And there the king is but a beggar! Yes, now that has power! Concision at its work. Systole, too, has both the meaning of the heart's contraction and ejection of blood into the aorta raising pressure in the blood vessels, the P wave…and of course it's also a shortening of a word, not unlike elision in the slurring together of words or the syncope of eliminating vowels as in, In the beginning how the heav'ns and the earth rose out of chaos. See, do you hear that? Heav'ns. Heav'ns. He laughed. It sounds like a stifled slur, doesn't it? And he exaggerated, Innn the beginnnning how the heav'nnnnns…

She placed the drink before him. He still had the other glass in his hand. You're kind of happy, aren't you? she said.

What are we without joy? God gave us drink to show us that He loves us! He put the glass down and swept up the other in one smooth motion, lifting the glass in pontific decussation. Blessings, he said, blessings to us all.

Through the tilt-a-whirl streets and the cartoon people, the long shadows of the buildings climbing the lengths of their brothers like creeping vines of incipient rootgrip, through tourists with heads bent back to view the facades and the second story entrances into mid-air's nothing but what was once imagined with grandeur and then abandoned, where a street would have been but then never was because the regrade never reached its envisioned level, such are the remains of proposals and blueprints and investments and contracts, on through beer garden chatter and waves of perfume, through arguments and harangues and the honking horn traffic where he looked around for any other vital creature in the congregation, Get the hell out of the street you idiot! Yet he kept his hand aloft to them all, the patron saint of cyclones, and to all in his stumbling humble awkward blind benediction, blessings...until he stopped at a pair of legs stretched out on the sidewalk before him.

With exaggerated bow from the waist and squint and blink he finally saw the sign that read:

Homeless
Anything will help
Even a Smile
God Bless

My God, he said, looking down at the man with his legs outstretched, a pair of legs in filthy green pants with nobody inside them, a man wearing several layers of shirts and an olive drab coat open at the neck, the neck and the face burned deep, almost black, hair like a matted bird's nest with a tinge of gray not from fading color but from the dust of the world, a cup at his side held in a hand that did not grip so much as lay next to it, claiming by proximity ownership, though the cup, Jones saw, was empty. The eyes were closed.

Jones looked in with raptor intensity, closed his eyes, looked again. The man did not move, did not seem to breathe, and for a long moment Jones stared at him as people passed in fast motion like phantoms in a near yet other universe, barely discerning Jones and this man on the ground beneath him as if the two of them were invisible or only faintly visible on the periphery of the world the way thieves run through alleyways unseen or public workers cleaning streets disappear or the dead come to peer in on the living retreat again to their borderlands of gray. Was he alive, this man before him? Jones tried to steady himself to see if he could detect any motion at all, any sign of life.

Here, Jones said. Are you all right? His voice traveled up from the bottom of a well inside his belly and came out like a whisper through the pipeline in his chest. He cleared his throat and began again. Here, hey there, you, are you all right?

No reaction.

Hey! He leaned down closer, putting out a hand to nudge the man or maybe try for an artery and check for a pulse. Hey. Are you...

The eyes opened, barely.

Jones squinted. All right? Okay. Hello, there. You seem to be...you should... Then Jones wobbled himself, losing focus for a moment as his outline wavered, then he locked back in again and patted down his coat and said, here, something for your cup.

He reached into his pocket and pulled out its contents and looked down into the confusion of rippling ground with its warp and weave of sidewalk plates like serpent scales overlapping, swelling and deflating with some regularity as he lost his hold and spilled what was in his hand on that maze of shifting earthskin. Then he caught himself and looked hard into his empty hands. He checked his other pockets and found toothpicks and business cards and something that looked like money that he directed towards that cup with some difficulty, tilting himself forward with his legs set apart, his hand wavering towards that narrow point of cup below, a shrinking target, as if it were retreating from his approach so that he almost lost his balance again and said, Now wait! Then dip and cantilever once again, this time fingers plunging into the cup and sticking there, then releasing his grip. He lifted his hand and the cup came with it. He lowered the cup and shook his hand and the cup came free, landing perfectly upright on the ground. A mid-air transfer between fast flying planes could not have been accomplished with more precision. He put his hands back into his pocket and pulled out what was left though in spirit now he was tuning into the next moment and oblivious of any money that might be falling out.

There, he said. What's your name? His voice sounded like a crooner singing through an old victrola. Your name?

Nothing.

Hmmm. Hey, my friend. Can you say…what's your name?

One eye opened, then the other. The man's mouth moved, but no sound came.

Jones leaned in closer. What's that? I didn't quite hear.

The mouth moved again, and this time a whisper came through as if from another space, Arl.

Arl? Is that it? Did I hear that right? Arl? Is that a name?

The eyes closed again, and the head faintly nodded.

Are you sleeping outside, my friend?

The head nodded again.

It's cold for that, I believe.

Nothing.

Jones kept looking at the man. Was he drunk? Was he starving? Probably both. So little life seemed to emanate from the form below. Jones said, There's a shelter down the street here, I believe, a mission. I've seen it. He pointed in the direction. Good Hope, or Good Shepherd. A Mission. You probably know about it, though.

The man had drifted off.

Watch out someone doesn't steal that money, hey?

Nothing.

Jones backed away. He turned, momentarily lost, his direction confused, trajectory broken, his destination unclear. The buildings seemed to blend like snakeheads in a pulsing pleorama with fangs erupting from the cornices while shadows dove from rooftops only to evaporate before striking the ground. He heard laughter and great turbines working below the street. He felt alternate waves of heat and cold coming in cross currents from the four directions. A face appeared and resolved itself before him with pictish grin turning ghoulish and sneering with gorgon hair and a mouth wide open as if unhinged to devour. Then it was gone. Distorted voices came from passing vehicles, upper floor windows, long echoing calls, and he realized from a place deep in the mind that he had crossed a border and was treading vulnerable in a terrifying current in which everything he perceived was permeated with subtle and collective tributary intentions and not all good along with projections from his own subconscious sprung free or maybe everything around him was appearing now with filters stripped away that normally preserved a stable and coherent condition. Everything was possible and everything was real. Buses swept by with long metal bodies that flowed and stretched like rubbery balloons with shuddering orbs within. Robed mendicants appeared searching the rubble for stones they tossed in a heap in the street while others of their kind converged and struck at the rocks with metal pikes with each strike sending out brief and flaring sparks. What a spectacle! Jones marveled at the absurdity of it, at the artistry and poetry as well as horror and confusion, then leaped from an oncoming trolley sliding by silent and leaning off its gleaming rails. Electricity jumped through the air. Everything was happening at the same time. He stood in the midst of it looking up into the folds of sky full of shadow forms falling like black leaves that broke like breath across his face there in the middle of it all as Gropius of Arcadia swept in with big boom chest and flea circus and bright mind waves of Pleroma. Hello, Mr. Jones.

He walked on tiptoe along the thin wire of the sidewalk. Walking will realign me, he said aloud or thought. Walk breathe walk. He chose a direction, and in this case any direction would do, and he walked. He kept on walking and the motion was a sobering act of repetitive choices, falling, catching himself from falling, footsteps through a foamy blur that became more distant as his own breath increased and the sound of his own breathing rose in his ears until he passed from that whirlwind of whatever whiptailing behind him and emerged at last among ferry horns and one lone seagull cry.

As Jones steered his way through the palm fronds of a few ideas that wanted to surface but kept diving back into the undertow, appearing just for a flicker like seal heads poking up and looking directly at him, seeing him in a way that makes him think they're considering him and considering his position and proximity and whether he's a threat or embodiment of ineptitudes from there in the deep waters while he with little spider legs runs frantic, and then he came upon an opening. It was that time of day that could be any time of day. Why, what have we here? he said, staring into the cloacal aperture of ground opened up before him, cut like an incision in a cadaver bloodless and clean, feeling like he had seen this before. Had he seen this before? He had seen it before, like something worker men were at, say, laying subway track or sewer lines, but there was nothing of the sort going on here, now. No, this was of an entirely different nature, something out of the science fiction books, a gateway, yes, that's just what it was, just that, down into…he leaned out over the hole, weight balancing precarious, rocking back and forth with a delicious thrill of catching the fall, because down below there were hints of acetylene and smoke and hook lights and miner's caps, but not the kind of apparatus that was up to regular street work, or maybe he beheld a glorious obsidian river blending oblivion and light, the blissful Hippocrene once again if only he could reach it and take a luscious sip, and yet again it was changing, a thing peristaltic and reptilian, an ouroboros with scales of myth-wonder. Upon which scale are you, dear shadow? More indeed riverlike and flowing with at moments bobbing to the surface emergent horse heads, whole horse carcasses it appeared in fact boiling up with lampposts and pickaxes and bricks and tents and timber crunched and splintered and poking up like cactus spines, why yes in fact he had stumbled onto the very portal between the unfettered spirit of the present and the pineal entrance to the skull's cathedral, the foyer to limbo full of discarded inspirations and memory and life's detritus jettisoned when the soul makes its perennial leap from one narrative bundle to another and comes up shaking mitred locks and gawping with primordial bewilderment while traveling through the arctic mind-bath of death's cotillion. Ah what a marvel! What a blessing! What a beast to behold! The kind of thing that inspires the shakers and the handlers and the riders and babbling seers of the tribes and the scribes in caves scribbling their visions for the holy cantors to sing to starving congregations. And why shouldn't he be given this gift, the revealing, the Sator Square, the palm at the end of the mind? Come at last! Hadn't he made his sacrifices? Been making them daily in the construction of sandwiches and the lave routine of hand and face, the examination of metric tables, the bustle and beehive navigations, the spin and clatter of the laundromat in apocalyptic spin cycles, the barroom suscitations and prescriptions and confidentialities of yes yes and oh yes, listening like a priest, singing like a goat, holding court, holding secrets, holding infirmary's head like an apple to the mouth of sad Adam stuck at the threshold of dull Eden and wanting to cricket-leap out of the thicket of a monotone…? Ah flesh. Ah, hidden desire. The cauldron of the human dream. Yes? And here before him now it was all opened up. And not in desert but in city center he stood, yes, verily at the navel itself. The very oracle, the well of conclusions and future visions down which one was cast to scream the mollusk mutton of the clutterbrain, dragged like a sponge through human days and decay and the mind at large with its cascade of prayerful and baleful complaining and begging and here so too Jones knew he was called upon to add his barbaric yawp to the rich earth ear and add to all the bilious conversation chatter and empty prattling on and on and so he opened his mouth and unleashed….Hallafactiouslatoranimockery I've been for you and you you see and me inside your blind bedroom feeling for a light feeling day and feeling for a way back to the child in the all body cast and casket and tree high above among the wisteria limbs and mystery winds and swaying haven't I? The game's afoot with rules cooked up by a zookeeper or a circus clown, the ground an acid bath to touch, each grass blade sharp as glass and dipped in curare…oh, no…swinging down so close those blades brush like tongues against the hair of the skin, like an acrobat, like a hero…yes, a hero, that's the very thing, pursued by the animus antiroo loveless gaming and questing but oh so ingenious! Hidden in rags and stupefaction. Outguessing and outflanking at every turn. How does he do it? It's maddening. It's unfair! He must have a map I can't see, after all, a mirror behind my head so he can see every card I hold, every diagram. Why did you do that? Rig the game like that? Give that creature access to every thread of thought and jurisprudence over every impulse? Dangling oh why yes like a marionette like a toy like a doll strung up over a campfire with sad plastic features melting globular and gloriously beautiful and revealing truth in blaze! Why make him in my image like that so I have to shatter the mirror to get out of the mess, the scene already changing as I fly right through the snapping jaws and the closing doors, your mad laughter following everywhere I go, nibbling at the nerves, biting at the toes, headlock in my dreams so I gnaw through my own bones to get away! Madness! Who conceived this sort of thing? Why? Why what kind of charade is this? Pain like a payment, like a passport into a country of fantasy makers who can only repeat the sorrows and sufferings they've seen through life after life so that we spiral and fly on the tornado's wings with farmhouse clap clattering and shutters flying off like burnt skin, good mother brisket knitting her charm into a pair of guillotines and sending us off on a forced march through jungle path classroom corridors and feudal trench rows, through blowtorch fields littered with the dead and small towns doused with sickness and company debt and anonymous foundry lives, through scry and atomizing, disintegration knowing…knowing it's happening while it's happening? Patient on the table without an anesthetic? And then the outer drifting observer disembodied and looking in all directions and especially down at versions of myself so that I am not myself and think why, I never was, never could have been at all, and so was it an illusion? Really? That's the great awaking? Just to dive back in and do it all again in another warped personality because I have to stand on the deck of the sinking ship and throw life preservers overboard to all of the sinkers with their shock faces and hands of ice so frozen they can't even take ahold of the rope, is that it? Sing your praises well and true and all the way merrily merrily and say why yes man is born of woman's womb and lo and so and here we go and knife blade to the neck, pistol to the forehead, it doesn't matter who has a hold, the reign of terror is the bubbling amber with a fly wide-eyed trapped and mouthing, Pleeeeease heeeeelp meeee, and it almost makes you laugh, shrinking down to the head of a pin with all the rest of the bumbling angels and the house cat swiping at your head to liberate you from all that dread you carried around like draft papers, like late homework, a kid in school sitting down to a test and looking around and knowing, knowing sure as judgment that the scrambled questions shifting on the page are moving targets, and I have no answers! I have no answers! It's radicals! It's reciprocals! It's a beast in a cage! It's the hypotenuse leg! When in doubt, sit and stare moodily across the room or out the window. Heh heh. He laughed a bit, expunged, expelled, outcast and free. And what did the oracle say? What answer returned from the whirlwind?

He looked up. A small crowd had gathered around him. Tourists. Children. People with backpacks and shopping bags were looking at him. A few were smiling. A few looked like they were getting ready to call the police. A few were pointing and talking to each other. Did someone take a picture? What was he saying? Yes, what was he saying? Had they heard all that? Ooh, he felt his face on fire, and looking up he saw the wolves and the rattlesnakes and the vipers all bending down from the rooftops. The sky was an open mouth. A storm was brewing. Had he started that? The thoughts in his head were turning in the same direction as the spiral blades of the clouds above. Surely, this could be no coincidence. He must have stirred up the heavenly gamelans and tapped into the engine of the great Macroprosopus. There would be consequences, without a doubt. He had better prepare himself. What are you looking at? he said, and he spat and snarled at them. Animal noises came from his mouth, it seemed, not the words he thought he said. Grunts and gurgles brought up from the depths. He had not fully re-assembled, recombined, reconstituted and amalgamated back into human form. The fur on his hands stood up and he swiped at the air. The people backed away.

What do you want from me? he said.

We're here for the tour, someone said.

What?

We were told to meet here for the tour.

What tour?

The underground tour.

We were told to meet in front of Doc's and the guide would start the tour. This is Doc's.

Jones looked up. The bulb lights were on, spelling out the name: Doc's. Why, it's broad daylight, he said. Someone laughed.

Are you here for the tour?

No! Jones said, then he took a deep breath. What tour is this?

The underground tour. The underground city.

Oh! Jones shot right through the fuzzy packing and shook his head and cleared the clouds. It all came back in bites. And it was all blurring as it formed. But he knew, he remembered. The underground city! Yes! No, I'm not here for that.

We thought this was part of the tour.

Me?

Yeah.

Funny, what you were saying, someone said. It was funny.

This was not what Jones expected. With both hands, he pressed against the top of his chest and pushed downward, smoothing the material of his coat. Then he cupped his hands over his mouth and with his fingertips rubbed his eyes then pushed his hands back across the top of his head, smoothing out the hair and resting his hands at last at the back of his neck, turning his head from side to side.

Well, he said. No, indeed, not here for a tour, and I'm afraid the show's over and hope you enjoyed the preamble to your journey. Charon shall be here shortly, and I'm sure your tour will be a most fantastical, historical lesson! Invigorating. Stimulating. Truly, an eye-opener!

Chuckles and laughter rippled through the little crowd.

But I'm afraid, Jones said, that I must now take my leave. And he conjured up a smile, looked down and tapped the ground a few times with his toe. This seems to be holding, he said. A few more people laughed, and he bowed slightly, took a deep breath and went about his day.

PART THREE

THE SAFE HARBOR

Descending into the lobby with her backpack on her shoulders, Sara passed through fetid zones of afterstink and crossed the black and white tiles worn gray in spots by the tread of uncountable feet and walked on through the ghostly traces in the rolling dust motes as light slanted in through the large front windows. Then she stopped and looked around. Through the windows she saw the people milling, stamping, smoking, laughing and taunting cars and strangers on foot who gave a good distance as they passed. Over on one lobby wall a silent television screen billowed its guardian of forever dreams and beneath it was a rack of dust-covered and sun-faded brochures and broadsides and maps. She looked through the less faded ones, pulling them back from their heat-fused stacks, and there came upon an advertisement for City College. She took the brochure and looked through its folded pictures of students in classrooms and courtyards, young happy smiling people beneath blooming jacaranda trees or bowed brilliantly over microscopes or laughing in undefined group projects. She took one of the maps and set her course through the doors and the cordrazine hiss of vapers outside.

She wandered the unfamiliar streets directionless at first, moving along in the bright liquid sunlight and absorbing scents and sounds and faces and facades. A trailer truck passed by loaded down with stacked cars crushed into bundles of flapping scraps. A siren sounded from somewhere not far off. People with their fierce intentions burning in their eyes flowed along the sidewalk while commuters in their bright machines came and went in a spectacle of rush.

She bought a coffee at a corner stand and sugared it and stood scanning the flow around her. Beautiful people flew by on rollers and bicycles or running on spongy new-tech shoes. They were bronzed and muscled and lightly clad in glowing shorts and tank tops like little nations with joy flags and mirror sunglasses, waves beaming private concerts yet moving like a synchronized parade of restaurant workers in black and white, hipster baristas with slouch hats, kids in jeans and tie-dye shirts, office clerks in slick suits and ties, silk blouses and rigid hair, construction crews on scaffolds and buildings under construction, bus drivers, cops with bullet proof chests and eagle glares, doctors, palm readers and beggars all, all in flux and flow, all together in the same dream and dreaming independently. What is the clerk to the doctor? What is the doctor to the woman carrying her bedding towards the next sheltered space? What mysterious relationship binds them all together and blinds them to their connection? This is what she analyzed at rapid speed as coffee hit her system and the impression of a paper bag caught in a little whirlwind hit her with acute terror and exquisite clarity.

God dammit, the man was shouting. God...dammit. And he jerked and threw violent punches into the empty space in front of him. He looked into a car stopped at the light, looked directly at the driver and shouted, What the fuck are you looking at?

Street torn open, workers in orange vests stood around and within a barrier of yellow ribbon with the word Caution repeated on it. Workers hacked away at old piping in an open dig with shards of concrete and a deeper hole that descended even farther than the network of pipes, a bottomless pit along which the workers stood on a precipice of dirt and stone buttressed with steel planks, a darkness below and eyes staring up like the very eyes of Adam. Smoke billowed and drifted over the street, and as it rolled over the heads of the people and the passing buses it took on the shape of a wan and gently blessing hand.

She turned down another street into a blast of sunlight and sulfur smell and smoke trails floating over swirling bits of paper and scattered clothing and helmets and canisters of expelled gasses and hand-made signs that said Stop the War and Eat the Rich and Madame Defarge is Coming for You. Banners of red white and blue with the face of a new leader stretched down from window ledges like Nostradamus beards over doorways open to darkness out of which faces peered radiating the vague unease of witness souls while old men sat with backs curved at an open bar with their feet in the light, their heads buried in the shade like a Manuel Bravo come to life.

The school appeared like an Aztec temple emerging out of a heat-wave with bricks flowing into benches and bicycle stands and wide courtyards converging in a set of rhomboid buildings. She wandered down the sloping ground that seemed to tilt towards a warm and radiant center square, and as she passed structures that looked like a nineteen-fifties vision of the future, she squinted into open doorways through which she saw classrooms, some empty, some filled with students. She walked along reading the signs with confusing split-numbered directions, and at last came upon a building labeled, Administration. She went in. The hallway was lit by flickering fluorescent lights, and she continued on until she came to an office with a sign over the door that read, Admissions and Records. She entered and found a room with three walk-up, glassed-in stations with signs hanging over them that read Registration A-H, I-R, Q-Z. There were no lines, no other people waiting to register, and she derived from this that it must be somewhere midway into one of the terms. She went to the first counter and the young woman there looked up and smiled and said, Yes, can I help you?

I was wondering when the next term starts.

We're on quarters, here.

The woman was a bright-energy young cultural guide with short hair and keen brown eyes and skin like a polished sunset, and she checked the schedule, found what she wanted quickly, and said, spring quarter begins on April first. Then she smiled a broad electric smile, April Fool's Day! What do you know!

April what?

You know, April Fool's Day?

What's that?

You've never heard of April Fool's Day?

I don't know what that is.

Where are you from?

South.

And you've never—well, it's a joke day. The day is just a joke, or a day for playing jokes, you know? You play a joke on someone and you say to them, April Fools, and it's just sort of understood, like the person you play the joke on is the April Fool. It's the first day of April. You never had that? Never did anything like that?

No. Not on one day in particular, she said, and she smiled.

Well, school begins that day. It really does, I'm not fooling. Are you interested in signing up for classes?

Sure. What do I have to do?

Well, first you need to fill out an admissions form. Then, you need to have your high school transcripts sent to us, pay your tuition and sign up for classes. If you want to apply for financial aid, complete that form too along with your application. In fact it's a good idea to fill out the financial aid form even if you don't qualify now because the cutoffs change all the time and you'll stay in the system once you apply. You never know!

Wow, that's a lot!

I know. It can sound overwhelming at first.

I went to a lot of different high schools, do I—

Just have the school from which you graduated send transcripts. You really only need to show you're eligible.

Okay. How soon do I have to get this all in?

You can sign up for classes until the end of the first week of the quarter. Transcripts have to be in by then, too. Financial aid forms have to be in at least three weeks prior to the start of the quarter, although sometimes they make exceptions. Check in at the financial aid office on that.

Okay. Thanks.

Anything else I can help you with?

No. That makes sense. Thank you very much.

Sure! We have kiosks in the library you can use to fill out the forms if you want. And if you have any questions about the forms or anything else, come back and either I or someone else here can help. There's also the Sydney system, always accessible. Thanks for coming in.

Ok. Thanks, that's great.

She went back out and wandered again through the buildings,

absorbing the feel of them, the energy, and it felt good. It felt right and balanced, and she went through to the courtyard and sat in the shade of a pyramid, poised with its point to the earth and its base to the sky, its shadow fanning out before her. And she took out her notebook and drew a sketch of the scene, the angles and shapes rendered down to a simple abstract collage, filtered and charged through her eyes and imagination into an Olympus of grace and light and beauty. Under the image she wrote a title: Geometry of Innocence.

They appeared a ragtag assembly of mystery players out of the heatwaves. How many were there? If she counted them one by one she'd say three, but then she would correct herself and say five. Definitely five. Maybe seven? Who could tell on a day like this? Even or odd, they were bright, too, light as angels coming right out of the sun and crossing the quad while she sat feeling inverted herself like the pyramids and their flying shadows, planning her life or trying to, calculating costs of supplies and classes and how much financial aid she could hope for and how much more she would have to pay and where she would find the money. And they zeroed in on her. That's what she would have said. Made a beeline in their dancing, prancing, miracle-wonder way of moving, linking hands, spinning, singing, One and one is two…Two and two are four…laughing all the way.

Their shadows reached her first, followed by the circle they set up around her like a wobbly amoeba. What a thought! She felt like a nucleus. How strange it was to feel like the center of something, so she closed her eyes and went inside. Maybe she would major in biology. Thoughts are things and this felt like a sign of something like biology was something she could understand because it made sense and it was real and touchable like the body she reached her hands to feel with its static sparks and electrified field. She got good grades in high school, so why not follow your strengths?

You a student here? She was a blond wisp of mist with a sun corona behind her head. Maybe she was their leader, or maybe they sent her ahead as the meeter and greeter.

Not yet, Sara said to the shadow of the other's face. Because that's what it was now, a shadow, a black hole where features should be. It was far too bright to look up and directly at them all individually. So she looked with a squint from the side. And they were moving and shifting and humming like high-charged electrons or a batch of bees. That was another thing, and it made sense. And it was almost predatory how they positioned themselves around her, as if light and shadow could be a weapon. She wasn't so much a center as surrounded.

You look like a student.

You look like a wayfarer.

You look like a child of God.

You look like a damsel in distress.

No, she doesn't.

She looks like a warrior.

A fierce warrior.

A warrior princess.

Sara lifted a hand to her eyes. Who was speaking now? It was hard to tell. They were all talking in many-headed unison or at least it seemed so. What strange characters. A hidden mind must be directing them and they are only appendages. She shook her head and smiled. What a funny little group to arrive like this and find her even if it was a bit suspicious.

What do you want to study? This time it was definitely the blond mist talking, singularly for sure.

I don't know. Science appeals to me, I suppose.

Science is dead!

Science is a lie!

Science is a trap!

Science is a slippery slope.

Science got us into this mess in the first place.

There's no hope in science.

What about your heart?

Yes, what about your soul?

What?

Their collective laughter sounded like a flock of starlings.

Science is beautiful, she said, but then it struck her: it's not something you have to defend.

This is beautiful! And their arms started swaying up and down and around like an octopus undersea. And who could say it wasn't beautiful?

Come on!

Come with us!

Come this way!

Why did she follow? Why not follow? They were calling. They were young and free and strange and completely unexpected. They were having fun, and they invited her, and she wanted to feel what they were feeling. Whatever it was. This was new. It was a new sort of thing, and it was electric and fascinating and energizing. She could feel her hands tingling. Why not? One and one is two…Two and two are four… She even felt herself singing along in her head. And off they went in a morphy group that she was now peripherally joined to wandering loosely into the world at large.

They crossed the street and then crossed a parking lot. No plan was set or said, no huddle or conversation, they simply divided, as if it were naturally time, with sparkling trails of angel light strung between them like stands of spiderweb as two went off by the dumpster and the rest headed toward a little food store. For a moment she hesitated. Then she followed the ones going to the store and through the ring-a-ding of the door and into its cool, air-conditioned interior. And that's when the show began. And so, without discussion or even looks of knowing they subdivided once again, now going like allele pairs in several different directions. Two went up and down the aisles. Two went up to the counter, laughing and singing. And two went back to the refrigerated glass doors. Sara stood there. What was she to do? She was an audience along with the clerk who stood bunkered behind his glass-partitioned counter with a bank of security camera screens behind him and a look like this was going to cost him no matter what. And yet, whatever they were doing seemed to put a spell on him too as they sang and danced and laughed and all swirled back to the refrigerated glass doors and plucked up each of them a block of ice and lifted them like babies and carried them up through the aisle again in pairs. Someone put a block of ice into Sara's hands. What a cold heavy weight, and yet it felt good. What was next? She followed, but instead of going to the counter to pay for the ice they all walked out of the store. And once outside, the other two came over from the dumpster with their arms full of cardboard boxes.

Aren't we going to pay for these? Sara said.

With what, dear Liza? With what?

They laughed and laughed.
We pay with goodness and light.
We pay with our presence.
Money is a lie.
Money is the root of decay.
But won't we get in trouble?
It's only water.
Trouble all the way!

Laughter, and once again the group gathered into itself like a thing of one mind that knew what it wanted without having to say it. Sara followed, holding her block of ice. How could they get away with this? This must be a trick. Someone must have paid or else the clerk would have tried to stop them. Wouldn't he? But she hadn't seen anyone pay. She looked back at the store, but no clerk appeared to be coming out, no shouting of hey, what are you doing, bring that stuff back here! It was after all only water.

They went back the way they came, back to the school and back through the courtyard of pyramids and through to the back of the school to a hillside there that they climbed in single file. At the top of the hill was a mission church with stucco arches and belfry and shadowed garden overhung with bright red bougainvillea. Mourning doves in the eucalyptus trees cooed their coded cries with a sharp uptick like a question followed by three short answers. What were they saying? Yes, what were they saying? Everything was up on its hind legs talking. On the grassy hilltop the players all set down their blocks of ice and tore down the cardboard boxes and passed around broad sheets of cardboard. Sara received hers and watched as they each took their piece of cardboard and laid it on top of their block of ice. What was this all about? They sure seemed to know what they were doing, like they'd done this before. And it seemed pretty simple, so Sara did the same thing, and with them she climbed onto her block of ice, kicked off with her feet as all together in a line they went sliding fast down the hillside riding their blocks of ice.

At the bottom of the hill they slid to a stop or tumbled off laughing and chasing down their ice. Oh, this was fun! And joined to that weird group of mystery people, Sara hiked back to the top of the hill with her ice and rode it down again. And how many rounds they got in, she couldn't be sure, but she was covered in grass and laughing and wet and feeling something she'd thought forgotten and feeling a part of something at least for the moment that was lovely and free and fun and like nothing she had ever experienced before. Was this what the world was really like? They rode and rode until their blocks of ice melted down to lumps they could no longer ride.

When they were finished with their play and the hillside was streaked with slicked-down grass, they left their melting blobs of ice and sheets of wet cardboard there at the bottom of the hill and wandered off and away, singing, dancing, an amorphous thing Sara followed for a while, not quite in or part of their group anymore though she felt an open valence invitation to join. The players were twirling ahead of her, but something snapped, something went off in her head and she stopped. What was it? What was stopping her? This she couldn't explain. She watched them, but she didn't follow as their group moved on, becoming one large shadow that wobbled and wavered like a jellyfish disappearing back into the sea. And so the afternoon swallowed them up. And she went back down the street to the school and through the long shadows of the inverted pyramids in the courtyard. What was that? Had that all really happened? How did they get away with it? It was like a dream, and she didn't know if she wanted to wake up.

Now students were coming and going to their classes, and Sara stood in the courtyard watching, wondering. Which room would she be in at some point? What a place. It felt like a home, sort of. At least, it felt like a place she wanted to belong. Maybe. But it was all still out of reach. And again she heard the mourning doves cooing. It sounded like each one was making the exact same sound. Could that be? Why the unison? If they were each making the same sound, what was the point? No warning. No courting. No appreciation of light. That couldn't be called communication at all. Not a chance. So then what was the point? It made about as much sense as these upside-down pyramids. And what were they supposed to mean, with their shadows like black sleeves on the ground? Still, it was fun. It was all fun and mysterious, this place she had arrived and the people in it. Like a dream. And so she looked down and tapped her foot several times on the ground to make sure it could support her weight before she took one hesitating step and then another and headed back to the street.

Once upon re-entering the hotel, she crossed paths with the man named T-Bear. He saw her and recognized her and stopped her with a warning palm upraised and almost but not quite touching her shoulder. And he said, What are you doing here?

She smiled, bemused. Was it a joke? I just got back from the community college, she said. I'm thinking of taking a few classes next quarter.

Oh! That sounds like a great idea, he said, and then he asked again, But why are you here?

What do you mean?

I mean this place, here. And he swept his arm as if to indicate the world, but she knew he meant the hotel, which was still a question she couldn't answer, so he took her arm, lightly, and pulled her deeper into the lobby and out of the worn track that lead down the hallway and eventually to the room where she was staying. He was smiling, but his eyes were narrow and severe, one of them milky and seeming to turn back towards an inner light. His voice was soft, however, almost a whisper so that she had to lean in and consciously listen to hear him. I've lived in a lot of places, too, he said. And originally...I had a sister a lot like you, I think, she was smart and read books. She wasn't always so nice if she was mad about something. I think she was mad about things I couldn't see. But she was smart, and she went to school and was headed for degrees and could have done anything. She was good at math and good at understanding science and she could recite in alphabetical order every musical play she had ever read or seen. She swore when she got nervous. But then something changed, and she dropped out of school and moved in with me for a while. She said she wanted to live in the real world. She wanted to work like real people and get real jobs like as a waitress or a secretary or temp worker like real people do. She kept saying that, like real people. I said, what do you think you are, Pinocchio? And it was okay for a while, you know, because we were just kids really and it didn't matter, I mean that's how I thought at the time, but after a while, after a while she was only partying and all that mattered to her was partying. She could do anything and seemed to be able to take it. She seemed to, but we were kids. I saw it change her, physically. I saw it in her spirit like a flame dying down, and I told her, but she was getting farther away inside herself and couldn't hear me.

I don't do drugs, Sara said, and maybe the pride-sound in her voice was not quite what she meant because she only wanted to tell him the truth.

It's not just that, and I hear you, right? I hear you. Going to college, that's good. And I'm nobody to tell you what to do. It's just the people here, the people you're with...

You mean Jack? He's not a saint. I know that. And look, you don't know me. You don't know where I'm coming from. I mean, I appreciate that you're concerned about me and everything, really I do, but I can take care of myself. I've taken care of myself my whole life. My eyes are wide open.

Good. Good...not trying to disrespect you in any way. But I know some things you don't know.

About Jack?

Yes.

So?

He's not who you think.

That's it?

Trust me.

Tell me something I don't know. What's he done? What am I supposed to watch out for?

Him. You just watch out for him. And if you're smart, you'll get away from here and him and you won't look back.

Or what, I'll turn into salt?

That's it, that and the city will go up in flames.

She smiled and reached out and touched his arm and said, Okay.

In the room that night, Jack went around from table top to window ledge and placed and lit many candles. The room seemed to waver and flicker here and there at its fuzzy edges and somewhere not quite seen as candlelight fluttered across the walls. The sounds of the street wove into the sounds of music coming from various rooms in a warp of worlds overlapping. T- Bear's warning was in her mind still, and perhaps in some ways it even sharpened the intensity of her desire.

You look beautiful, Jack said to her, pulling her towards the bed. And he whispered it to her again and again as he kissed her and drew his fingers along her throat.

And they lived in a dream drifting on timebergs making love and watching the light of day roll through the room like a slow lonely apparition wandering around looking at things and then retreated back into evening as the streetlight on the other side of the window illuminated their twin forms on the bed there as she watched the cool jewel moon cut scythewise through the narrow space above and between the razor teeth buildings. Then they rose and went out and walked along the streets and avenues and dipped into bars and book-stores and little curio shops, but they never went far from the room, as if the room itself were following them and all its previous occu-pants and indeed every occupant of every room she had ever inhab-ited had come along for the ride only now to be slowly exorcised by the fire of their lovemaking. She felt herself slowly and consciously remolding herself through these energies, claiming her world in a way she had never been able to claim before, and the sexual perfor-mance was a part of this in a pentecostal and methodical yet myste-rious way she couldn't articulate yet which became more and more certain as it was urgent and plaintive and bold. And he became some-thing both more and less as she embraced him, his face constrained in some violent and painful battle, his methods of love sometimes tedious and sometimes malevolent, as though in the act she were able to catch a glimpse of something beneath the skin, the mask removed, the self, the true self poised there for the briefest of moments when he lost control and appeared to her a demonic and hungry explosion contained in the hyper concentration of a single sad human urge for something outside itself. And in the calm of a break during which they lay beside each other naked in the pale light he said to her, Do you ever wonder why we met each other?

Why?

Yeah that's what I'm asking you. Do you ever wonder? Do you ever think maybe that bus driver didn't stop and let me on the bus, and that maybe you rode on and we never met?

It's hard to imagine, now.

I think that's because it could never have happened any other way. If you can't even imagine it happening any other way then it was meant to happen.

You believe it was fate?

I believe that things happen in a way that...things happen and there is no other way that they could have happened, ever. If that's fate, I don't know then I guess I believe in fate.. I mean, maybe there's another place where none of it happened the way it did and we went right past each other, but we can't be there, too. You know what I mean? I wonder sometimes if we start out in a room and write it all down, you know, like a plan of what you want your life to be and then you go out and get born and live it and it's like you planned it, you know, and not? We make it up a little and that goes into the ingredients with the other souls writing out their list of life demands. But I also think our minds are way over-developed, and we have these imaginations that dream up all kinds of possibilities but the truth of the matter is things just happen in a way we can't explain and never will explain and because of that we have to accept this world as the only way it could be. Maybe that's fate. I don't know.

Well, you're the one asking what if the bus hadn't stopped.

I know. I can't help it. Wondering's like an addiction, but what good does it do?

Well, she said, and she let her arm rise in the light above her, turning her hand so that the bones of her wrist twisted slightly. I think the imagination is our highest power and our greatest gift. Look at what's around us. Nothing would be here if someone hadn't imagined it. Someone imagined a home here, then built it. Someone else imagined a road, and then there was a road. Another person imagined a building made of many rooms; now we're inside that building. Every moment we're imagining the next moment and what we'll do, what we'll be. We imagine ourselves into the future and that's where we arrive.

That's beautiful, he said.

I know.

But there's only one problem.

What's that?

Death. If we're imagining ourselves, why are we imagining getting older, getting sick, dying? Why aren't we imagining paradise all the time? Why aren't we imagining ourselves beautiful and happy and peaceful forever? It seems a lot of people are imagining a whole lot of horror, war and ugliness.

That's true. People are imagining horror and war and disease and sadness. Maybe we don't completely control our imaginations. Who knows, she said, pointing up at the little moon in her three-quarter burn between the high-rising snouts of stone, who knows what imagination makes up the stars or the wind or the waves pounding in our hearts?

She met Annie Dupree when she went to pay for classes. They stood in line together, and Annie struck up the conversation first, saying she wanted to take Modern World Literature, Creative Writing, and British History; saying she had taken Philosophy with an absolutely brilliant professor who was young and good looking, but unreachable it seemed by some purity of ethics or existential vow; saying she herself would take nothing that did not excite her soul, that did not fit into the trajectory of her dream to write and act and sing; saying that the only way to live was to seek your bliss and follow your instincts and to never compromise, much; saying that in fact she had become a Buddhist after taking a religious studies class in which she learned the four noble truths: that all existence is suffering or dukkha or the feeling of everything going away, that suffering is caused by clinging to life and the things of life, that all suffering can be ended, and that the way to end suffering and attachment and clinging to life was to follow the eightfold path. And the eightfold path meant holding in your mind the right view in life with that spark of aspiration to the highest nobility of spirit, speaking only rightly according to that aspiration, and of course acting according to that aspiration, working only to end suffering while causing no suffering by your actions, and keeping on with that effort, trying for what you know to be true and beautiful, thinking this way with all your heart and mind, which is a battle itself. By this path you will reach bliss, Nirvana, an idea she was still not certain of, wondering if it meant simply the end to one's karmic debt and the cause-and-effect path, a complete cessation; or a unification with the divine wow which itself, according to some traditions, was either total unification with the godhead or an apotheosis which resulted in the sensation of sameness while the individual spirit still retains its separateness in the Atma and Brahman relationship, or as St. John of the Cross said, she said, a feeling as though one gazed upon god through a glass so clear you cannot see it. The more she studied the existentialists the less she was convinced that they had come up with anything new, other than a tendency to be both more complicated and at times utterly simplistic, but what philosophy or religion didn't have contradictions? In fact, Annie said, she was wondering now whether or not a philosophy of contradiction could not bridge all the metaphysical structures, for what is sameness without difference, difference without sameness; or better yet, that contradictions and paradox are the problems all religions strive to reconcile: life and death, good and evil, spirit and body...ahh, so much to know, and what does it really get you? And then there was Kant's categorical imperative, with its principle that all human beings have something like a conscience, although she had doubts about that sometimes, especially when she watched the news. As a great writer once said, know all philosophies but keep them out of your art. And that was exactly what she was going to do, learn as much as she could, but keep it out of her poetry and her music and her painting because she loved all the arts and thought it a moral flaw to think you have to choose between them.

They went to a coffee shop and talked and the more coffee Annie drank the faster she talked, and it seemed that she already had so much knowledge, so many ideas, and had read so many books, Sara couldn't understand why she needed to go to school at all.

Did you learn all this in one class?

Oh god no, Annie said, and she lit up a cigarette and pressed her lips together and blew smoke through her nose and tilted her head to one side. I've always been interested in Hinduism, Buddhism, Christian mysticism, the Kabbalah, Native Ceremony, Taoism, Zen, Tantra, Yoga, all the Western philosophers from Plato and Aristotle, Aquinas and Meister Eckhart to the three stooges of empiricism: Locke, Berkeley, Hume, and also because they were fun, occultism and Tarot. I've got a deck; do you want me to read your cards?

Sure, I suppose, Sara said, but what she didn't say was that growing up as she had predisposed her to think of things like Tarot cards as dabbling in evil. She couldn't be sure when, but she had let go of that fear somewhere among the anonymous rooms they inhabited fleeing from her father's nightmares.

Annie took out the cards and handed them to her and said, Shuffle them, and while you're shuffling them concentrate on what it is you'd like to know, or on some good memory, or a problem you'd like to solve or someone you love or anything at all, or else just clear your mind and be as blank as you can be and when you're done set them on the table.

She shuffled the cards. They were oddly sized, larger than playing cards and awkward in her hands as she tried to smoothly blend them in the arched, double-handed shuffle she knew how to do. The cascading coalition that was supposed to result from this action came out as a quick, flat collapsing of the stiff cards falling together. She did this several times, smiling, embarrassed by what she felt must have looked like gracelessness, and handed the cards back to Annie.

Annie picked up the cards and dealt them out in a pattern with several in the center and some in a row to the side. Then she began to read. Mmmm. Mmmm, she said, looking them over and taking a few drags on her cigarette. Wow, she said, You have some powerful forces operating in your life.

Sara looked at the mysterious cards Annie laid out. She didn't know much but recognized the death card because what else could a card with a skeleton swinging a scythe be for, and she felt her gaze fix upon it.

Now the position of this card is pretty important, but don't let it frighten you. This Queen of Wands is at your center. That's a powerful image: fire, attraction. I think with the Moon over it like this, though, you seem to be battling through something, some fear that overlays you, in this landscape, right? That looks pretty sinister, some darkness, the night, the midnight, the dark night of the soul in a way, something you might even be generating yourself, some illusion you're clinging to, I'm not sure, or the illusions that others have of you. That's possible. I think it really means that you are coming through some conflict, a struggle. A man is involved, here, in the fourth position, represented by this Knight of Swords. He is opposed, here, in the sixth position by, well, the lovers. That's interesting, and it seems good, especially with the Strength card in the seventh position. See here, this line that ascends? Look, you've got The World, sometimes called the Universe card, in your tenth position. That's very good, very positive. Big changes coming, or you're right on the verge, but good. Your feminine divine is manifesting and this is what it looks like. That's where you are. I think you've got some...well, here, the fifth position, this is your conscious state and you've got the Nine of Pentacles, see, the woman here with the falcon: that's your goal, a spiritual power sort of setting up the future against the sixth, here, which is the lovers, right, which would seem like a change in a relationship and it very well might be, but by the greater arrangement I think it has more to do with an internal relationship shifting, but the Nine, that really seems to mean you've got to rely on yourself pretty heavily, although it does lead into this ascent, and yes, this card here: The World, yes, that's the outcome, no doubt about it, right here in the tenth position which is the culmination, a kind of ending before beginning again, and the Fool right before it, well, that makes sense because you have to step off, you know? Any great journey begins with a single step, but don't misunderstand, the Fool doesn't mean you're foolish. It makes sense that that would be your last obstacle because it's really what you think of yourself. The Fool is the beggar, the vagabond, but that's freedom. The Fool is free, a free state of mind you need if you're going to start an adventure! But sister, I think you have some...well, some miles to go before you sleep.

A rebirth, huh?

Sure, in many ways. The choices you make along the way are important of course. Are you planning to move?

I just moved out here.

And now you're starting college. That's a move, too, right? I would read it that way. Is there a man with whom you've had any kind of conflict?

You could say that. But who hasn't?

I think this shows you coming out of that, Annie said with a nod of her head. Definitely. Rebirth makes a lot of sense.

Rebirth sounds good.

When she returned to the apartment building, she went fast down the hall with her head straight forward and was on her way to their room when she passed an open door and someone inside called out, Hey, come look at this.

She stopped and looked in, a little apprehensive. Quince was waving a hand at her and sitting on the bed with his legs crossed. Mark was sort of playing a guitar while a young man stood by who himself looked apprehensive. She stepped just inside the door but didn't fully enter the room which itself was full of human reek and a sink on the right stopped up with the faucet dripping into reddish-brown rusty water that gave off its own poisonous odor. Quince had his bare feet up in his lap, and he was picking under the yellow toenails with a paperclip, the smell of his dirty extractions adding to the putrid fumes. Mark, a matted and clotted mess of tangled black hair and gray teeth and patchy cheek stubble, plucked at the strings of the guitar and said, What do you think? This guy wants two hundred for it. Do you think it's worth it?

She glanced at the young man who stood with his hands behind his back, almost but not quite touching the wall, not quite touching anything at all in fact, looking edgy, jittery, like a sped-up version of a visitor out of his element ready to bolt but in need of the cash. It looks like a nice guitar, she said, but I don't know anything about guitars.

It's not what it looks like that's important, Quince said. It's how it *sounds.*

And Mark plucked a few more strings, but it was obvious he didn't know how to play it.

I don't think Mark's playing it to its full value, then, she said. Quince burst into a good laugh that sounded more like someone had performed a heimlich maneuver on him.

Mark sneered. Do you play? he asked her.

I told you, I don't know much about guitars.

Then how would you know what it's supposed to sound like or what its value is?

She shrugged and said, You asked me.

She was about to turn to go. Let's hear him play it, then, Mark said, and he pushed the guitar towards the young man who hadn't said a word yet and still didn't speak as he took the guitar and held on his knee with his foot propped on a chair. He began to play, strumming a few chords, plucking out a song that was both simple and beautiful.

It sounds nice, she said. The young man played a few more chords, brought the picking up to the higher frets in a kind of finale, then stopped and held the guitar up gently, turning it slightly and sliding his hand down the neck and strings.

I'll buy it, then, Mark said. And he got the money from his dresser and gave it to the young man who then perhaps a bit reluctantly gave the guitar to Mark. She again turned to go when she heard Mark say, You ever get it on with a man? And at first she thought Mark was talking to her, but looking back she saw that he was addressing the young man. Quince sat there grinning on the bed behind him, and then Mark laughed and pointed at her and said, Or are you in line for the little girl?

She didn't say anything after that but left and continued on to her room, their voices diminishing as she walked away, or rather Mark's voice diminishing since she still hadn't heard the young man speak at all. And she went back to her room and sat on the bed shaking but not from fear. The slick walls oozed their amber roach plasma full of little ticks and hisses. And so she waited as the light faded, and she left the room light off and let the darkness seep through the windows along with the pale glow of the streetlamp which had at one point had a romantic and erotic energy to it but now was a drained husk-hue. She waited, thinking the door was going to open at any moment and Jack come smiling in. But he didn't come in, and she waited, feeling herself draining, drifting, though she mildly resisted it, into a deathlike sleep.

He didn't come back. It could have been days she waited, and when he did return and she tried to ask where he had been he just grunted in a kind of horse snort and said, With some friends. When she got angry and said he was a liar, he rose to twice the height of her anger and pounded the walls and kicked the bed apart and stormed out, leaving the room in a shambles. And so he became a new monster, gone for days at a time, coming back sometimes drunk, sometimes penitent. He never struck her, but she began to fear that that time was drawing near, and the memory of Annie Dupree's Tarot reading superimposed itself on her impressions of the daily unraveling of this new version of her world so that she made sure now every night that her things were packed in her bag: the few clothes she owned, the notebooks, and the gun her father had given her, predicting one day she would need to use it.

One night another man with another name entered the room. She was alone and writing in her journal and he came in through the door and closed the door behind him and stood there smiling or more rightly grimacing and looking her up and down as he reached down and began to undo his belt.

What the hell are you doing? she said, closing the book. She remained right where she was.

He said I would find you here, the man said, and that was all he said. She could smell him now, the stench of sweat and alcohol. She stood up, her heart pounding with new fear.

Well, he was wrong, she said.

You look just right to me. I give him fifty, so you come on now. His pants were down and he was holding himself with one hand while the other tried to pull a pant leg off of one foot. She stepped forward and pushed him, and drunk as he was he fell over heavily as she stepped around him and out the door.

She went down the hallway and down the stairs and through the lobby full of its clowns and freaks in their huddled groups like manic jostling creatures in a funhouse. And she walked out to the street where other men called out to her, nasty vicious tongues and lurid requests, offers, prices, saying what they wanted, saying what they'd do. She pushed through, even as she felt them reaching for her, felt them grabbing her arms, felt them pulling at her shirt so that she had to yank herself free as though from gorillas. She moved on with her gaze straight forward, pulling herself free from that whining vortex of dripping souls as she walked on down the dark street.

She went to the coffee shop and sat in a booth alone. The few people at the counter looked over and watched her as she slipped down and covered her face with her hands; then they turned back to their cups and food and conversations. The waitress came over, a heavy middle-life woman with a black wig and black eyeliner and a blast of vast indifference in her eyes. Do you want a menu? she asked.

Just some coffee.

Coffee, the waitress repeated and shook her head and punched a green order pad back into her pocket as she turned and went back behind the counter. A few moments later she brought the coffee over and without even looking down placed the cup on the table and turned and then herself was gone. Sara settled into the obscurity of the booth and breathed more slowly and felt her heart beating more slowly as she sat with her hands around the coffee cup, staring at the reflection of the light overhead as it wavered and then locked into stillness held there in black liquid.

And there she sat in a kind of black liquid, motionless for over an hour, thinking, where will I go now? I don't have the money for a place of my own. Where will I go? How much money do I have? The bus fare, the college tuition. Can I get that back? I can, I think. I need to have money or...but where? And her mind swirled around a navel of possibilities and then came nestling back like the light in her cup to one center, one solution, one place, which was nothing more than the spot she occupied right now. But how long would this last, and when the moment ended, then what? She still had to return to the room. The man was most likely gone by now. The image of the fool emerged in her mind, open, face tilted back as the feet stepped toward the precipice. Zero.

She didn't drink the coffee, didn't even taste it. She paid and rose with her mind in a far-removed space of awareness, watching as she rose, watching herself move past the other tables and the old waitress who didn't even look over, didn't even notice her as she went out the door, and she felt in her mind in its distance completely invisible.

She walked back along the same street, but it was as though she had been transformed at the molecular level, sub atomically, or something in her gaze was revved up, the way she presented herself, shielded, tough, for no one said a word to her now as she passed through the pantheon of woebegones, and the thought came to her again, I'm invisible. She passed the knots of clustered people smoking and drinking and talking, and they neither stopped nor turned nor looked at her. She went back in through the high double doors and into the warped lobby. She heard a loud hissing sound like an air duct blocked with paper. She moved in dreamy slow sure steps, fearless, calm and distant, back to the room. The door was open, and Jack was there.

The moment he saw her, his face came alive in a thousand ways, and he stood almost on his toes and shouted into her face, You little bitch! What the fuck do you think you're doing? Who do you think you are? Huh? What are you doing here? You tell me because I don't see it? Are you bringing money in? Are you? Are you even trying to help out here? Or is it all supposed to be on me, in your mind? I want to know. Huh? Is that the way you see it? Well, fuck that! That's right. I said, fuck that! And he shook his head and grabbed both her arms and held her rigid and said, if you don't bring in money, and I don't care how you get it, but if you don't then you are *my* bitch, do you get that? If you're too fucking stupid to get your shit together, then I have no choice but to do it for you, do I? Do I? And he let go one hand and pulled it back coiled and then swung and punched her hard in the chest. She fell back, at first unable to feel anything, except that she was unable to breathe. He reached down, striking at her again as she lifted her arms to block the blows. Then he began kicking her, and she doubled over and rolled back and found herself pinned against the side of the bed. Then he kicked at the bed and at the bureau, knocking it over, and in that moment she reached under the bed and got a hold of her bag. You think you're getting out of here now, you little whore? he said. Is that what you think? Ha! That is not going to happen. You have a debt. Do you understand that? Can your mind comprehend that? What a debt is? How it is incurred by taking, that's right, taking and therefore disrupting the balance so that you have to make it right. Do you understand? Your side of the balance is deficient! You owe! It's your responsibility to set the scales right, and if you don't, then this is what happens. Do you understand? And around his head floated an armada of black shadow blobs that seemed to feed and bloat from the air coming out of his mouth.

From her distant vantage point above the room and looking down through the transparent walls, she commanded her hand to go into the bag, commanded it to find the gun, commanded it to bring out the gun and point it at him. She didn't tremble, but when he saw it he began to laugh.

Are you serious? That's your next move? That's what you came up with? You think that changes the balance? Huh? You think that scares me? And he lifted his hand and spread his fingers like claws and bared his teeth and hissed. And she pointed the gun at his chest and squinted her eyes and pulled the trigger.

He smiled, looking not at her but at the gun, a strange expression of knowing and wonder drawing his hands in towards the black burn mark in the middle of his shirt but careful not to touch it, looking down at it and the little bit of smoke that coiled up as though his soul were already leaving. Then he stepped back and sat on the bed. His mouth opened, but he wasn't speaking now. If his eyes could speak, she thought, they would have said, good. They would have said, that's better. He looked like he wanted to sleep. He lay down on his side, his head on the pillow. He looked at the floor. He seemed to be holding his breath. His chest was still and black-red with blood. His eyes were open but blank. He didn't move at all.

She rose and collected the last few things left in the room that were hers and put them in the bag. Then she went to the sink, ran cold water and dipped her hands into it and cupped it to her face. She did this several times, then simply held the water in her palms until it stilled and there held the reflection of the overhead light. She let it go through her fingers, turned, and cultivating her force walked out and through the hallway that like a gallery held in every door another head that leaned out but didn't seem to see her.

She walked on through a field of night terrors, devils, twisting neon and cars passing and flowing around her in confusion. She had no idea at all where she was going. Isn't this how the fool starts off? She was utterly lost. But she kept to one direction, west, like a homing pigeon, her eyes wide with feverish and rapt attention. So much sound around her with the cars and drones and people and construction and destruction, it was like a roaring of the void, and when at last she came to a place where the road ascended and then curved into a cloverleaf of exiting and entering rush and howl of the freeway, she stopped and turned and lifted her hand, thumb outstretched toward the oncoming cars.

A forest green pick-up truck eventually pulled over and stopped, and she went up to the door and looked through the window and registered the face inside of a man who looked back at her with an apprehension that nearly matched her own. He waved for her to come on in, and she opened the door and climbed aboard. She had just barely closed the door before the truck was in motion, throwing her back against the seat. Sorry about that, he said. Someone was coming up on us from behind there pretty fast. I had to get moving.

That's all right, she said, and she put her backpack between her feet, pouch open just enough to get her hand in and grab that gun if she had to, and buckled herself in.

I'm Arl, he said. Where you headed? I'm heading north. Where you headed?

That's fine, she said.

What's your name? he asked.

My name's...and she hesitated; then she said, My name is Michelle.

They moved with the fast flow and she leaned her head against the window and felt comfort in the motion as she watched the lights of the city diminishing in the side view mirror.

HAWALA

Summer drifts in an endless time blur of days and nights hot-moving through open windows and building up and sweltering and squatting in rooms so that sleep is nothing but sheet-wrestle with marelocks and heat-hallucinations full of shadow moving presences the likes of which he can't quite comprehend yet beholds in flashes of night hags and reapers and ghostly headless cloakmen disappearing under direct gaze to take up residence in pine trees and pet cats and leaving just a retinal hint of after-images rolling across the cave walls behind fluttering eyes. Mosquitoes buzzed the nights in the dark above his head, and Gabriel played a losing game of lying in wait for them to land on a bit of exposed cheek so that when the horrible buzzing stopped and he was sure the little blood suckers had settled down to feast, he slapped his own face to kill them. Rarely, he got one. Usually, they flew away and then returned with that high-pitch buzz just as he was about to fall asleep.

Summer rolls in waves of heat so the house porch is a ship prow in a doldrum sea haze and cloud nebulae floating deep into empty space. One afternoon in the basement den of Peter Andrews's house where they watched an old-time movie called *When Worlds Collide* with believing fear of the cataclysm of crashing planets as the last few people boarded the ark ship beneath a sign that said Waste Anything but Time. Would the quick-built ship lift off? Nothing like it had ever been made before. They were over the weight limit. Not everyone would escape. And the crippled benefactor trying for the metal doors rose from his wheelchair on atrophied legs and took halting quivering steps that made it look like his will was willing him to walk. The earth destroyed. People destroyed. And the ark takes off and makes its salvation run to the frozen planet crashing its way onward, survivors climbing out onto a cold dark ice world. Gabriel walked home in the bright afternoon with that hollow end-of-the-world vision permeating everything down to the hiss of the hot sidewalk and the muttering of the dandelions. Would it happen in his lifetime? The seas boil? The rivers die? People crawling after escaping ships, refugees headed into the dead of space? What a thing to contemplate after sitting in the darkness watching a movie on a summer day.

And then his sister said, You want to see a real movie? They watched *2001: A Space Odyssey*. The apes. The monolith. The crying voices! The slow beautiful ship, drifting in orbit, like a white skyborn dolphin. The moon and the station. The monolith. The Voices! The Jupiter mission. The computer, Hal, winning at chess. The breakdown and Pool cast out into space, wriggling for horrible moments with his dislodged air hose then still and floating. Bowman in the pod, going out to retrieve the body, cradling it in mechanical arms, gentle, heart-breaking. The slow dismantling of Hal and the sad singing of Daisy, Daisy, and the journey inward into the monolith over the rushing kaleidoscope landscape, the eye, the purple eye, the vision of the aging self in a cold white room. What was happening? Self beholding self. The strange reaching and then the unborn infant out of nowhere filling up the screen with its eyes. He understood very little of it, and yet all of it made sense, so that he would remember it scene for scene forever.

It's all happening out there in space with ships going farther out and the sky crowded with traffic and Earth just another port of many where he climbs one day into one of those ships and into his own liquid chamber of suspended animation and waking lightyears away and stepping out onto strange ground and breathing miraculous air and striding through low gravity atmospheres with each step taking him leaps ahead among aliens of every form so close you can smell their flesh and hear the ticking of their mandibles and not all of them friendly and not all of them monsters either but all far away as if he were stuck in the wrong system in a house in the middle of nowhere.

Summer jumping out of time with no beginning and the end was so far away it might as well be imaginary, and each day lingering late in a baked blue dusk so that who could say if it was ever truly dark? Gabriel rode the neighborhoods beyond the park, alone, through streets of big willow trees and pitch roofs with dark porches and rooms lit from within with doors wide open. Other streets with ranch-style all-window A-frames and light-collecting cell-plates and car husks on front lawns and the night gentle embrace of warm empty fields and blackberry and pine sap and cool water creeks as he flew into the driveway so dry the dirt puffed up around his tires as he skidded to a stop.

And then in the hot dry late season when the church holds its retreat, they're heading out to the island while their father stays behind, the ferry full of church group members heading up to the canteen to buy chowder and beer and hot pretzels and then out on deck playing guitars and singing and then sliding back into their vehicles as Gabriel and his sister and mother climb into the old bug with its missing passenger seat and hole in the floor and radio playing summer hits, rolling down the shadow road in the flutter of forest limbs to the campground on the bay with its a series of old cabins with driftwood nameplates like Cedar, Pine, Spruce, and Hemlock scattered across a sprawling compound of grass fields bordered by the forest, and after dumping their stuff in a room in the Hemlock house Gabriel's sister said to him, You know, Socrates killed himself by drinking Hemlock.

Not only did Gabriel not know who Socrates was or why he killed himself, he didn't know what Hemlock was. He was tentative and said, Why?

His sister looked cooly at him. You don't know who Socrates is, do you?

No.

He was a philosopher. And she smiled with the possession of knowledge she wouldn't share.

Families arrived unloading the contents of vans and campers into piles of duffle bags, suitcases, and coolers. Gabriel met up with Joe and Jerry and their frantic-eyed mother Kathleen fresh from a tune-up in the psych ward and their father who rode over on his bicycle in what seemed impossible time. Joe had on his black wooden cross, and for the first time Gabriel felt a pang of loss for the one he no longer had. They ate in the big hall and went up to vespers in the cedar grove beyond the rope swing and the volleyball court. The sun shot a side-eye on the minister as he preached about the voice of god and the quiet mind we need to hear it, so Gabriel listened to the conversation of the standing people-trees swaying on their spongy roots spread out underground and their murmur signals traveling the branches with secrets of water and light and conclusions based on lives lived in observation.

There were sign-up sheets for different activities each day: tie dye, pottery, model-making; or activities like hiking, canoeing, swimming. On the first day, Gabriel went with Joe and a small group of other kids on the forest hike, the trails with wooden signposts pointing off to destinations like Eagle's Roost, Lookout Point, Pioneer's Cabin and The Cemetery. Gary the youth group leader stopped to name the banana slug and the salal and lion's mane and other things on their way to the Eagle's Roost midway on the Pioneer Cabin loop. Everybody stay within sight, he said before they set off. I don't want anyone getting lost.

The hike up to the lookout was steep and rocky. Joe and Gabriel kept to the back of the group, and at one point Joe reached down and brushed his hand against a nettle and then drew it back laughing, saying, Ah-ooh, that hurts! And then he laughed and did it again and said, You try.

No way, Gabriel said.

Go on. It doesn't really hurt.

Gabriel stuck his hand out and touched a nettle with his fingertip, but nothing happened.

You have to touch it with the back of your hand, Joe said.

Gabriel brushed the back of his hand on the nettle and felt a sting. Ow, hey! he said. Joe laughed. Gabriel rubbed his fingers over the spot but it just kept stinging.

I heard the Indians use ferns to stop the sting, Joe said, and he pulled off a fern branch and rubbed it on his hands. Gabriel yanked out a branch of his own and brushed it over his hands, but it didn't seem to work. Then, he reached down and pinched a small handful of dark wet dirt and rubbed it on the sting and that seemed to cool its intensity. He held out his dirt-dark hand.

Try that, he said to Joe.

Joe reached down and grabbed some dirt and spread it on his stings. He looked surprised. How'd you know about that?

The lookout tower was off the trail, and they climbed the stairs and stood at the top with a view going out over trees to the north and the west, the flush forest rich dark and dense, and ravens flew in and out of the trees caw-cawing, light shining on their black wings. Something in the mind goes where the eye looks, and Gabriel leaned against the rough wood railing while a feathered awareness went on over the brush of treetops and the stroke of airwaves in a kinetic and volatile wonder flight to the edge on a vague smoky tether then boomeranged back to the hollow bone fragment of his head enchambered in light shafts coming down as Gary told them about the children who had wandered off into the forest maze and were never found again but who appeared from time to time to hikers who might see them like timid deer in the trees calling for help but when the hikers wandered after them they became lost themselves.

The pioneer cabin itself was not much its former shape but fallen moss-covered timbers in a gully and buried away from the world so it seemed now nothing but a sad and lonely even frightening place to be. The fate of its occupants was a mystery they speculated on with various scenarios:

Bears got 'em.

They probably starved.

Yeah, they ran out of food.

They must have just abandoned it.

Maybe they're buried in the cemetery.

Who could live here?

I'll bet Indians got 'em.

Yeah, they were killed by Indians.

Scalped.

The cytoplasmic sky split into clouds drifting timeless and Gabriel hopscotched juggernaut shadows flowing over the grass and went up to the craft cabin where they were making tie dye shirts and a leather lanyards and whistles and models like the submarine with see-through side and intricately detailed interior bunks and torpedo room and command bridge, and he constructed a spaceship with a lift-off top that exposed control room and sleeping quarters and cargo hold, these toys and imaginary play dangling futures like fishing lures. He met his sister and his mother for lunch, but otherwise he didn't see them much at all. Sometimes they ate with friends instead of with each other, and after dinner there were always ping-pong matches on the covered porch outside the dining hall, then it was back to the room at night to sleep in the cool cabin with its old wood smell of years gone, but during the day they went their own ways. Gabriel's sister and her friends took over the macramé class and with the older kids dominated the volleyball court. One of the older boys approached him and asked if she had hair yet. Gabriel didn't say anything and the boy just laughed and went away.

Most of the time, he was on his own.

One night Gary took them on a night hike up to the cemetery. They each brought a flashlight, and Gary wore a miner's cap with a light on it. The woods were pitch black dark, and their lights disappeared into nothing. Gabriel pointed his flashlight up into the branches above and saw the light fade out in the gray tree limbs. They sang She'll be Coming Round the Mountain When She Comes, and Gabriel wondered who 'she' was. When they reached the cemetery, they sat on the ground. Sometimes, Gary said, people get buried alive. It doesn't happen very often, but sometimes people with sleeping sickness look like they're dead but aren't, so they're buried alive, and if you listen you can hear them scratching in their coffins. Listen.

The children leaned down to listen, and as they did, Gary screamed, Let me out! They jumped alert and laughed from that adrenaline jolt.

Each day contained an hour of silence in which nobody spoke. This was the time to listen to God. And so people lay in the shade or walked silently across the fields in a slow-motion moving prayer.

Cottonwood seeds drifted through the warm afternoon. Gabriel was at the oars, now that it was his turn. Joe and Jerry were hanging over the bow carving lines in the green algae with their hands. Then

Joe said, I brought some firecrackers. Gabriel turned. Joe pulled them out. They were wrapped in a packet of red paper.

Where'd you get them? Gabriel asked.

One of the big kids let me have them.

He let you have them?

Yeah.

He stole them, Jerry said.

That's a lie.

Does he have any more?

Nope.

Joe had matches too and lit the firecrackers and tossed them over the water trying to get the timing right so that they went off right before hitting the water. Some blew up in fast blasts of wadded paper scattering over the water. Some went in with a sizzle. An adult on the shore waved and called out for them to stop that.

On the last night the local tribe had a salmon bake for them on the beach. They gathered and built a bonfire and made sand candles by pouring melted wax into holes they dug in the beach and skipped rocks on the bay and ate fried bread and smoked salmon. Gabriel wanted to ask someone if they knew about the Crow, but nice as they were to throw this party there was a distance between them and the church group, even if everyone ate together and played together and all later went to a dance at the tennis court where there was a mix of native songs and dances and popular line dances with rows of people dancing in unison and illuminated by the court lights. Everyone learned a few new steps. Cookies and punch were set up for the kids in a little tent. Adults smoked and drank sitting on benches at the edge of the court.

When the retreat came to an end and Gabriel and his mother and sister packed up their things and loaded them back in the bug, it was the first moment Gabriel felt a change in the light, a change in the air, something silver flashing at the edge. Then they climbed into the car and drove across the wooden bridge and out onto the fluttering road back to the ferry dock where some of the others were already there boarding the ferry boat with them, and as they pulled away and the land fell away, one of the younger men sat on deck with his guitar playing altered comic versions of church songs and pop songs as people laughed and sang along.

They got home and were carrying things back into the house. Gabriel's parents got into a fight. It was brief and it was hushed, but it was severe. Then his father got into the car and left. His mother sat on the front steps and crossed her arms on her knees and sighed and laid her head on her arms. Gabriel and his sister waited nearby in the yard looking at each other, picking grass blades, waiting. After a while their mother said without looking at them, without even lifting her head yet knowing they were there, Go inside.

They waited in the living room and watched through the doorway as their mother sat on the steps under the eaves with the creeping shade of the yew trees. The sun withdrew and the light faded. She didn't move. She may have cried, but they didn't hear her. They sat a few feet within the door and waited and didn't move either.

At last, their mother rose, turned, and came into the living room and said quietly, calmly, Your father and I are getting a divorce. The slow, almost imperceptible time of summer seemed to hold for a moment longer like a relative in the doorway. Gabriel's sister began to cry. Gabriel, like hearing another person speaking through his mouth, seeing himself from outside himself said, I had a feeling.

A few days after their father left he returned but only to get some of his things. He took one carload. That was it. Clothes and some paints and brushes. He left everything else behind: all his woodworking tools, his left-over and some incomplete easels, paintings, pottery, wood sculptures, furniture, books. He took so little, it was hard to tell by the look of the house and everything in it that he was leaving. But when he climbed into his car, Gabriel went and stood before him in the driveway with his arms folded and would not move. His father sat in the car and looked at him. They faced each other for a long moment, but Gabriel resolved to hold his ground and hold his ground he did until his mother came and pulled him away, not struggling or crying but resisting with his weight until at last he relented and the car moved down the driveway and his father left for good.

Like a miracle, the hedge called him over. Not regular talk. Then something caught his eye. A glint of smooth plastic. He simply reached in and took out a sword. Hedges shivered with magic possibilities after that. No one among his friends claimed the sword, and so it was his. And that was a precedent upon which he built a notion of possession: what comes into your hands is yours by right.

He tested this first with Peter Andrews's carved wooden sasquatch slingshot. He simply snatched it while playing at Peter's house and hid it under his shirt. At home, he kept it hidden so that he wouldn't have to explain how he came to possess it, and it took on a weird kind of secret power that worked on him like poison, making him ill while it was the favorite of all his things. When guilt finally overcame him, he smuggled it back into Peter's room and never let on he had taken it.

Then it was the drugstore. He took candy. It was easy. When no one was looking, he took it. The feeling was the purest beautiful sensation of fear, excitement and control he had ever felt in such a way his heart raced as he moved through the aisle making his selections. He felt his face must show his intent, but he could make a face that concealed it. He imagined a face of unquestionable innocence and beamed, even lingering after pocketing some toy or package of candy, looking around as though he were intending to buy something when already he had the object he wanted to steal. Later awash in a mixture of shame and pride he was unsure which one was stronger. Sometimes he would secretly return things to the store. Sometimes if he waited a while those feelings faded from his consciousness, which became another lesson: for some things the conscience has a time limit. And always there was a part of him that watched himself in amazement at his boldness and amazement at his audacity and amazement at his greed and the abilities that grew more subtle and refined as he became more practiced at it. His room became a dragon's lair of treasures he could share with no one, show to no one, and play with only in secret and with the fear that he might be caught with them and be twice guilty and twice charged. It was a strange direction for him to go, he thought to himself at one point. And all the while he continued going to church with his mother and sister he felt himself divided and the two parts ranging farther and farther from each other until one could only call out like a brother on a loud seashore to the deaf other heading into the unknown.

Then he became cocky. He bragged to a few friends that he could get them whatever they wanted. He didn't tell them he was going to steal. He let them wonder how he would manage to do it. Did he have money? They stood on the corner up the block from the drug store. What do you want, he said. I can get you anything.

One of the boys glared suspiciously at him. Why?

If you want it.

Anything?

Sure. Toys. Candy bars.

All right, candy bars.

Yeah, what kind?

He went down to the drugstore and walked in and looked over the greeting cards and self-help books and lotions and potions and then went up another aisle and put four candy bars into his pockets and turned and went back and looked over the cards and books and other little dumb trinkets again. Then he felt his pockets move and turned slightly as he looked down and saw two hands pulling the candy bars out. He looked up and saw the old woman who ran the drug store standing behind him and holding the candy bars. She reached down and took him by the hand and dragged him back behind the counter. And though she had steel-gray hair and a pair of glasses on a chain and a pink sweater vest with the drugstore logo on it, she was stronger than he was and yanked him and pushed him down onto a stool and looked hard at him and said, I'm going to call the police.

Wait! he said. I'm sorry. I won't do it again. I promise.

Oh, I've seen you at it before, she hissed.

Please, he said. I promise. But he couldn't inspire her mercy. She went to the phone and dialed.

He sat there in terror. And after a while his friends came in and saw him there and laughed and pointed and said,

What happened, Gabe? You rob the place?

What are you sitting back there for?

What's the matter, you caught?

You boys go on, the old woman said. Get out of here now.

Gabriel said nothing. His friends left. He sat with his head bowed.

She didn't call the police, though. She called his home, but his mother wasn't there and so he had to wait and wait and wait until she answered and at last could come down and get him.

When she led him out of the store, he couldn't speak. She asked, Why did you do it? But he could make no words. His eyes were wide and his body tingled, but he could say nothing, could barely move himself. He allowed himself to be guided to the car, and there he sat silent and dazed and ashamed as they drove home.

The gray rain days slithered back in snickering through the fall air. The bamboo rustled like a thousand tongues against a thousand teeth. Gabriel stood in the doorway of Timothy's apartment, bare walls radiant with smears and the smell of the place too like unwashed clothes and toilet and the kitchen a sweet rancid stench of plutonium water to the brim of the sink with dishes stacked with days of dried grub and little towers of black plumed tentacle hair mold and open cans and garbage canister overflowing with its bloom of waste. The two younger ones, foster children Timothy's mother took in for extra money, sat on the couch bathed in the blue electric television light, their faces dirty and their mouths hanging open with dull hunger gone to boredom. Gabriel was aware of things in new ways though still on the border where play could override the perception of their squalor.

The row of bamboo trees swayed hypnotically and whipped in gusts of wind, and Gabriel hovered in the doorway looking out, unsure whether to stay or go. He held a toy car in his hand, the kind that sparked when the wheels turned, but it had the lifeless and waning allure of things held too long, and he was on the verge of chucking it.

The sounds of radios and voices and children crying rose out of the surrounding apartments. He couldn't actually see into any of them, but they were close and separated by thin plywood scrims, each with a little cement patio exactly like the one he stood on, and from behind the building came the constant waves of traffic. He turned and went back inside and down the stairs to the windowless room below. It was brightly lit by a bare white bulb, and the white linoleum floor glowed, and there Timothy sat with his own cars, skittering them across the floor. He was a thin kid with wild black hair, and like his foster brother and sister he wore filthy clothes and had perpetual grime about his neck and the joints of his elbows. He was a quiet, gentle boy and kind so Gabriel became a friend to him, although Timothy was a significant year younger. Their friendship arose only because they walked home from school in the same direction, and one day Timothy invited him over to his house. He never actually met Timothy's mother. She was a nurse who worked nights and so slept through the day, so play had to be quiet, and there was a kind of veiled anxiety in the way Timothy and the two others moved through the apartment.

Gabriel stood looking down at the younger boy from the lower grade, thinking with some unease that he was here partly by choice and partly by chance. By chance they walked the same way but by choice he joined Timothy. These are two ways things happen. He could have made another choice, and that thought made his mind jump back and back to a moment in the first house he lived in and not the one now when he would have been maybe two, three and he went to the back door with its corners full of spider webs and opening the door beheld the sun and for a moment thought he'd come from there. He walked out into the grass. Colors of the lawn and flowers, the bees and the dragonflies and the clouds and sky suddenly lit up. Certainly he'd seen color before, but this felt like the first time. And looking back, thinking back now he remembered thinking then and remembering in a vague way that he was somewhere before this. Had been somewhere before this house, this family, and he knew it and hazy could see it in his mind. And as he watched Timothy playing he knew his own days of play were falling away. Already, something had departed.

I think I'm going home, Gabriel said,

Did my mother wake up? Timothy asked.

I don't think so.

They went up the stairs. The two other children didn't move or look at them or take their eyes from the television screen. Timothy turned the volume down and went to the door of his mother's room and opened it slowly and looked in. Over his shoulder, Gabriel watched and saw in the darkness a lumped mass like a bear in hibernation beneath a blanket on the bed. The floor was covered in heaps of clothes and alcohol vapor drifted out like a cartoon cloud with pointing fingers. Timothy closed the door gently, keeping the knob turned until it was fast in the jamb.

They stood in the front doorway. The bamboo hissed and swayed. The rain came in sputters. Where's your dad? Gabriel asked.

I don't know. He never comes around. Does your dad live with you?

Gabriel picked up a dry bamboo stick and whipped it through the air. It whistled faintly with each swipe. My dad died.

How?

In a plane crash.

Gabriel walked out through the patio and onto the street and crossed the double flow of traffic and climbed the hill through the apple orchard where the grass swept across his knees and soaked his pant legs as he approached the house buried in the trees where an old drunk lived, a man they taunted though they never saw him. He kept his windows shaded. They tried to spy him out, but he never appeared and gradually it became rumored that the house was abandoned but maybe haunted. Then stories arose that he was seen up by the children's hospital and that he was hunting children and burying them under his house. They snuck up onto the porch and peered through the windows, but they never saw him inside or out. As Gabriel passed, he swept his bamboo stick through the grass and watched the place but kept a wary distance.

Idle time. Torpor of screens. Sounds and images. Problems, engagements, lusterless characters, even the ones he built himself losing their allure, draining down to the quiet room and a fly at the window. Where was everyone? And sometimes it felt like a stranger came up from behind and gave a little push. Or sometimes from the side, like jostling through a crowded street in winter against people heavily padded in winter coats, waves like currents changing directions even pushing down from above or up from below like walking through water, it was amazing his feet stayed on the ground...but what were these buffeting crosscurrents and why did they feel like living things? The ground, the trees, the air and clouds—inside them these currents flowed unseen of old and even in the rusted plow stuck in the blackberries at the edge of the field and the leaning trappers shack with chains and snaptraps and vials of wolf bane and deer musk and a little hole in one of the planks that if you put your eye to you get zapped and vaporized in an instant, old rock thinking and remembering its way back down slow days to nothing much and uncountable moments in the incremental movement of light like a troll under the bridge who knows every little secret yelling and no one listening, or aquatic and cocooned in oceans and deep lakes, or something more science fiction or mythic, still wind...not a leaf moving and on the scent of cold bay sea tendrils and sunken things dark down under and the beach music with beautiful people so you can almost feel the sidewalk sizzling and the ice cream truck song warbling somewhere near yet not a spear not a stitch of wind or breeze... nada but still that jostling of woolly bodies like a crowded platform to the last ship on waves upwelling so his head and shoulders bobbed like a diver, a nudge here a nudge there, something.

The return of the school routine and the music teacher leading them in a sing-along of Lucy in the Sky with Diamonds. The girl with kaleidoscope eyes. Six times one is six, six times two is twelve, six times three is eighteen, six times four is twenty-four...the rote, and the only way he managed it was by song and rhyme. Drear windows in obscure wet rainwater flow of fall and all the wet coats hanging on hooks in the closet and the steaming heaters hissing and radiating and fogging the window glass and floorboards warped from generations of passing feet.

And they came and asked him: How did your father die?

He died in a plane crash, he said.

His mother took him to a psychologist at the church, and he sat in the little office room in a big leather chair with his hands folded on his lap and one knee bouncing imperceptibly. The psychologist was a tethered goat man with a smile turned inward and pulled down by his nose and a wooly sweater with sleeves pushed up past his eczematic elbows. He wore big black glasses, and a few straggler hairs fought it out over his dome. The window behind him was open to the sound of traffic and light streaming over his shoulders that made his face a shadow. How's school? he asked.

Fine.

What subjects do you like?

History.

Who are your friends?

Walt and Peter and Giorgi. I play with them mostly.

So everything's pretty okay at school?

Yeah, pretty okay.

And how about at home?

Fine.

What do you like to do?

Watch TV.

And your sister?

She reads a lot.

Do you like to read?

Not really.

So, how about your parents? They're getting divorced, I hear.

Yeah.

How do you feel about that?

Sad, I guess. But okay.

Gabriel went to see him once a week for a month, and the psychologist asked the same questions in different words but waited a little longer for Gabriel to answer, and Gabriel gave the same answers in different ways, keeping guard, knowing he was on the verge of trouble beyond which lay more scrutiny and possible punishment if he didn't make a good show now.

Driving home after that month of sessions, his mother said, So, what do you think about seeing this psychologist?

It's okay, he said.

Do you like talking to him?

Sure, it's okay.

I thought you might want to have a man to talk to, since your father left. Has it helped?

I guess.

Do you want to keep on seeing him? His mother seemed to be giving him the option. He had to be careful. If he answered too quickly it might set off alarms, so he didn't respond at first. He sat still in the new front seat they'd gotten to replace the one that was stolen.

I guess I'd rather not, he said. He looked straight ahead. He could feel her looking at him, but he didn't look back.

All right, she said. You don't have to if you don't want to.

He held himself and didn't say a word. They drove on, and he thought, no one ever asked me about the lie.

And so the time of school moved by in a watery dream with one day looping into another with minor variations. In the rain the playground was a low shriek of soak-em, a version of dodgeball, with headshots off limits and teams picked with political precision and each side its own minor nation of killers whittled down to two and then one player, sometimes the least skilled vainly dodging as the prisoners screamed, Come on, catch a ball, the best-skilled players like Chris and Peter and Georgi and Brian jumping and screaming the loudest because they knew given a chance that they could win, and out of the barrage of shots and dips and dodges Gabriel stood the last player on his side as someone on the other side threw the ball at him and missed. He retrieved it and threw it back and missed. And then the ball came at him and he caught it. The prisoners on his side cheered. One came back into the game. The glory was beautiful.

At noon on Wednesdays the air raid siren blew, but where once children might have been told to duck and cover or huddle to one side of the gym or lockdown in a room, now, no one stopped their play, though the sound infiltrated every game, every body, every nerve so that a moment comes when almost all hands go to the ears and cup them and lift away and cup again, playing the sound against the head so that it becomes a wavering doppler sound while some kids scream along with it.

In drizzle rain that floats and swirls and shades of gray and light that comes and goes, Gabriel walked home from school with kids before him and behind him all homeward marching as well, and he passed houses he knew down to the slope of grass and lean of porch and snap of dogs, homes of children, homes of ghostly shut-ins, the geography of everyday walking to and from school that becomes as familiar as your own heartbeat so that no matter for good luck he ran his finger along the green metal railing in front of the Sorensons' house where Paige lived who one time invited him to come into the backyard to play, and he was there only a few minutes before her father came out and said, Paige, your cousin's coming over. Then turned to Gabriel and said, You better head on home, now. Three's a crowd.

Charlotte was walking ahead of him. For some time he had loved her. Anonymously he gave her coins or flowers or little rings or bracelet trinkets from the store, wrapped in school paper upon which he wrote, From an admirer. He hid them in her desk when no one was looking. Then he watched as she found them and looked around trying to figure out who this admirer was. When he finally revealed himself by adding his name, she looked at him and smiled. But her parents made her give all the gifts back. They said I'm too young to take these gifts, she told him. He smiled anyway. So he stopped giving her gifts. Now she was walking ahead of him with her umbrella over her shoulder, and for no reason he walked up behind her and pulled on her elbow so that her umbrella tipped and water came down on her head. Hey! she said, but she was laughing as he jumped back and she whipped around swinging the umbrella out and brushing his eye with its metal tip. He stopped and put his hand over his eye. She stopped and stared at him. Then he lowered his hand and saw it was full of blood. She saw it, too.

Oh! she said. I'm sorry! I'm sorry! And then she ran away.

He walked home, his eye bleeding and tears flowing a little but not from crying because he felt very calm. He went up the steps and into the house. Hello? he called out. No one answered. He sat down in the kitchen and called his mother at The Beef and Brew where his mother was a waitress. Someone answered, and he said, Hi, is Molly there?

Yeah, just a minute.

Hello?

Hi, Mom?

Yeah, what is it?

I got hurt coming home from school today. A girl hit me in the eye with her umbrella. It's bleeding pretty bad.

Oh my god, honey. Are you all right?

I think I'm okay.

Can you see out of it?

Yes.

I'm coming right home. Stay there.

Okay.

He went upstairs to the bathroom and looked in the mirror. His face was covered with blood. He was shocked by how much blood there was. He turned on the tap and ran the water and took a wash-cloth and soaked it in the water and wrung it out and placed it on his eye. The coolness felt good. Then he wiped the blood from his face and tried to open the eye and could only get the eyelid to lift slightly. It wanted to stay closed, but he forced it open with his fingers and looked and saw that it was bright red along the upper half. His vision was obscured, as though looking through bottle glass. It wasn't painful but felt scratchy like something was in his eye, and he wondered if a piece of metal got under the eyelid. He couldn't blink it away. He put the washcloth against it and sat down on the edge of the bathtub and waited for his mother to come home.

He heard the car arrive. Then he heard the door open.

Gabriel? his mother called.

Up here.

She came up the stairs and stood a moment in the bathroom doorway.

Oh honey, she said, and she sat down beside him and stroked his hair back. Let me see.

He pulled away the cloth. She looked into his eye and then gazed at him. Let's get you to the hospital, she said.

As they drove, he looked out through his one eye and felt a strange post-adrenaline calm. It was all right, now. Everything was all right, even if his eye was damaged. He covered the other eye and made himself look through the injured one at the watery world of trees and traffic and street lights and people on the sidewalks, as his mother tried to slip between the other cars to get ahead. At certain angles he saw brilliant shards of light like diamonds in the sky.

What happened? she asked.

A girl hit me with her umbrella.

Why?

I don't know.

The doctor took him right in and laid him down in a reclining chair and dimmed the room lights and snapped on a spotlight and pried open Gabriel's eyelid and looked down through a magnifying glass at Gabriel's injured eye. Hmmm, he said, and Gabriel could feel his breath against his cheek. There's a small cut in the eyelid, he said. An abrasion on the cornea. We'll have to stitch the lid and see what happens with the surface of the eye, but it looks like it should heal okay without any problem. How's your vision through it?

A little watery, said Gabriel.

All right. Well, let's get started, the doctor said.

The doctor slid over on his stool and gathered up a tray of utensils in trays of blue liquid and prepared a syringe and inserted it into the inner eyelid. Soon the eye and eyelid and cheek and face went numb. He stitched the eye, cleaned the site, and placed a cotton bandage over it and taped it down. Gabriel was awake through it all but somewhere else through most of it. Well, the doctor said, rolling back on the stool and standing up. Keep it covered and don't get it wet. Come back next week and we'll have a look.

Thank you, Gabriel's mother said.

The doctor helped Gabriel out of the chair and said, All right?

Gabriel nodded and shook his hand.

As they drove home, Gabriel felt the balm of his mother's love and her overflowing concern and absorbed it deeply.

When they got home, he went into the living room and turned on the television and sat down to watch. His sister came down from her room and looked at him.

What happened to you?

Nothing. I got cut on the inside of my eyelid. I got one stitch.

Does it hurt?

A little.

Hmmmh, she said. How can you watch that show?

My other eye is fine.

You sure? Then she went back up to her room.

Gabriel called out, Mom, can I eat dinner in here?

Sure, she said.

A phone rang.

He watched the show, a rerun, with the familiar villain's sinister laughter as he dropped the secret agent into an underground maze full of trap doors and booby traps. The agent stepped into a room and the door slid closed behind him. He turned, but the door wouldn't open. When he turned back around, he saw the floor splitting, opening over a pit of boiling acid. Soon the floor would be gone and he'd plunge into the acid, but the agent took out his gun and inserted a steel arrow into it and hooked a wire to the arrow and shot it into the wall on the opposite side of the room. He climbed up onto the wire and slid over the pit to the other side.

Gabriel's mother came into the room and went over to the television and turned it off. I just got off the phone, she said. It was the mother of the girl who hit you in the eye. She was calling to apologize. But do you know what she told me?

No.

She said you were teasing her and that you hit her.

I was just playing. I didn't hit her.

You lied to me.

I didn't hit her.

I want you to go up to your room. No television tonight.

But I was only playing.

Go.

He went upstairs to his room. He left the lights off, sitting in a shaft of hallway light coming through his door. He lifted his hand and felt the bandage on his eye. His eye was beginning to ache. He felt his sister in her room next to his. He could feel other presences, too, in the old house, especially the previous owner who took all his money out of the bank and buried it in the walls. He died, but they never found the money. Gabriel stood up and put his hand against the wall, sliding his fingertips along it, tapping lightly, feeling his way like a safecracker and listening through the wallpaper and plaster. The house was whispering to him all its little secrets. It was whispering to him about the money while outside the trees were swaying and throwing wild shadows on his floor.

Well, she said as they sat around the kitchen table, it's either going to be New York City or Berkeley, California.

Why are you going back to school?

Why a school so far away? his sister said.

They're the ones that accepted me. They're good schools.

How long?

It will only be for a year, two, two years. At most maybe three…at the most. Then, I promise we'll move back.

Three years?

One year, maybe two. So, New York or California.

New York in the mind was a TV city of building canyons and steam boiling out of vents in the street and random violence, killers, gangsters, and Berkeley was a complete unknown. But California. How far would they be from Disneyland? The sun was all over California. The sun was always in California.

I'm kind of hoping California, their mother said.

Definitely, California, Gabriel agreed.

Sure.

But what about our house? Gabriel said.

We'll rent it out to some college students. We'll pack the things we can't take with us and store them in the basement.

What can we bring?

We're going to drive down. Maybe we'll rent a trailer. A couple of boxes each, I suppose?

Like big boxes?

Just boxes.

Won't the people who stay here get into our stuff?

They won't do that.

Choosing California was a relief followed by dread as the time to go was nearing and the days changed into a new kind of fall impossible to slide out of and back into the floating unbound dreamy summer. Gabriel moved through the house and through each moment with the combined excitement of going back to school and the fear of leaving their home and moving to a mysterious place so that when he tried to sleep his mind continued building and boring through scenes of palm trees and beaches, swimming pools and movie stars, but the gap of the unknown his mind struggled to fill flickered like a glitchy TV station and made his stomach ache.

He packed as if they were going on a long camping trip because now they were only taking the Bug, no trailer, so they could only bring one box and a suitcase each. And it was a little sad dividing himself from his possessions and deciding what to take with him, even if at a certain point a clarity came so that once a few things were let go other things lost their value and went more easily, but what he kept became totemic: backpack, two books by Arthur C Clark because he liked the covers, a watercolor set and a chess set, his Bible, a desk lamp, a stuffed bear and a box of cufflinks and tie clips that belonged to his father.

Home was dissolving from within as they moved their boxes into the basement. They left the furniture where it was. They couldn't afford to store it. His mother found renters. And gradually, the day to leave approached, and the closer it got the worse it felt. Gabriel's anxiety grew, but it also came to him that this was a chance to renew himself, to shed thieving dark impulses and become holy once again. He would be a good person again, a child of God.

The intention was to leave by morning. By six in the evening the car was finally loaded with boxes on the seats and on the floorboards beneath their feet and suitcases on a rack on the roof. When they climbed in, there wasn't a space to spare. The idea of home and possessions now fit inside the car. When at last they pulled out of the driveway, the house fell away inside the long shadows falling across the lawn as sunlight strobed across their faces as they drove through the streets in the rose glow of evening.

On the highway, sparse traffic flowed. Gabriel sat in the back right, his sister on the left, with the clothes hamper between them that was filled in fact with clothes that needed to be washed. Their mother drove with her shoulders up in defense posture as trucks swept by and sent wind gusts that put their little car into swerve. To talk meant to shout above the sound of the road coming in through the open windows and up through the hole in the floorboard, but none of them said a word, and slowly the road took over as they crossed the first in a series of bronze rivers shimmering with snakes of light.

Then it was one town gone as another rose, the aroma of a pulp mill and last light shooting through a cloud until gradually the road became a lulling rise and fall as the engine droned into a daze.

Gabriel leaned his head against the window and felt his gaze slacken as they passed ragged Uncle Sam billboards with bible verses and abandoned villages and foothills loaded with darkness and empty fields and cows that stood motionless in empty fields as shadows pulsing against his eyes until he fell into a light sleep with phantom set designers sitting him on a bus in a city with someone he knew but couldn't see because the other was turned away as the bus made its way through a crowd of people who were standing and waiting, and when the bus stopped all the people including the other descended and Gabriel followed and tried to catch up or at least stay within sight of the other, but the crowds were moving all around him and he couldn't keep up and gradually couldn't see the other and was on his own and knew by dream logic he had to find a certain house, thinking I should have gotten the name then I could look it up, but now I'll have to go by instinct, and so he set off in a follow your gut direction and the streets rose steep and then plunged down through neighborhoods of half-built buildings and schoolyards like bomb sites with crumbled walls and graffiti on everything and streetlamps with rims hanging down and abandoned cars stripped of their wheels and doors and high-rise apartments with dark windows and empty parking lots as if civilization had lost interest and withdrawn and now the world was inhabited only by shadow forms like ghosts, if they weren't in fact ghosts, and Gabriel walked down the middle of the street which was now virtually impassable to cars, the ground roughed up and buckled, mounds of earth and more abandoned cars and trucks, some on their sides, and came upon the remains of what looked like a military installation with gun emplacements and metal gantries and ammunition bays, and he saw children running along the walkways above and more emerging from tunnel openings and swarming over like ants as he rushed on through the iron stanchions of a fallen tower bridge with water flowing below and through the concrete and metal bulwark and though he couldn't tell how to get across he knew his destination was on the other side.

They pulled into Ashland and drove by motel after motel with no vacancy until almost out of town they entered a swirl of dust and tumbleweeds and passed under the wagon wheel arch with blinking sign that said Frontier Inn with cabins that looked like buckboards and parking to spare. Their room had an orange door and two beds that sagged in the middle as if someone had been dropping bowling balls on them and a television with aluminum foil on the antenna that only got two grainy stations: local news and a gameshow. Their mother went out for burgers while his sister sat on one of the beds, her back against the wall and an open book in her lap. Gabriel explored the bathroom. It smelled like urine and disinfectant, one of the two only slightly stronger, and even though there was a wrapper around the toilet seat one grizzly hair hung to the edge of the bowl. He picked up a paper-covered soap bar and unwrapped it and washed his hands and face. He picked up one of the overturned glasses at the back of the sink and sniffed it and ran the water till it felt cold and then filled the glass. When he drank the water tasted wrong.

He went back into the room and sat on the edge of the bed and looked at himself in a framed mirror on the opposite wall. The television was bolted to a wall-mount bracket, and the bracket was bent as if someone had tried to steal it. The walls had a strange snotty yellow texturing and the drapes and bedspreads and carpet were saturated with the smell of cigarettes. It felt like they were hiding out, on the lam, running like fugitives. The drama was fleeting. The hiss of cars and trucks passing on the highway came through the walls like ocean waves.

How far do you think we drove today? Gabriel asked.

I don't know. His sister was pretending not to watch the television. It was a medium mostly beneath her. She pulled her knees up and was all about her book. Occasionally she glanced at the television. Sometimes she scrolled several strands of her hair through her fingers as if she were reading a sacred text.

I bet we went five hundred miles.

Probably more.

What time did we leave?

Around six.

Gabriel tried to watch a gameshow, but the picture was fading in and out and other images crowded in with shapes superimposing. He tried other stations and got nothing. He adjusted the antenna and spread its coat hanger arms and found that doing that refined the signal, so he explored further by twisting the coat hanger and feeling his way like a dowser connecting into airwaves until something else appeared that looked like a cop show. I think I've seen this before, he said.

I'm not surprised.

Are they speaking English?

I'm not listening, how would I know?

Headlights punched through the windows as their mother pulled back up in front of their cabin. The door opened. Anybody hungry, she said as she came in with a bag of hamburgers and fries. She was smiling, but her eyes were weary and red.

I am, Gabriel said. She handed him a burger.

How about you? She said to his sister.

His sister grimaced and said, Hamburgers?

It was the only thing I could find at this hour.

She took one and looked at it like it was a prison ration and they ate sitting on the beds with the sound of the highway and the crinkle of wrappers and the static voices on the television.

They started out early and ate breakfast in a little roadside diner that gave out little game books, and the golden hills of Oregon rolled like ocean waves with sweetgrass scent flowing in through the open windows, the road rushing by below in a blurry gray of gravel and asphalt as Gabriel watched it through the hole in the floorboard. Reading the crossword puzzle book made him carsick.

Then his sister said, There's an Idaho.

Gabriel looked out the window. I see Oregon, he said.

That's easy, his sister said.

I see Washington, their mother said.

I see California.

That's the first one.

I see New York!

Hours of drone as Gabriel dozed in and out with eyes open closed open, slow in drowse as the world outside and the river behind his eyes merged in flashes and glimpses of towns like cutouts and riverbends emerging from blond hills and somewhere in there gazing becoming floating becoming hovering and going up and back along the road and out into field on field as a disembodied idea. A dark blue spider lake appeared. Then the Siskiyous rose up, and they rose slowly into them, the vehicle slow-laboring, trundling along at thirty miles an hour as car after car and big rig trucks swept past them. Scrag pines stood like vagabonds coming through the heatwaves, but there was no forest like back north. The land was sparse and dry. Occasionally far below on the drop-off side of the mount rivers flowed and trees hunkered thick on the banks. Then they passed the summit and the road descended and the car seemed to lift off the ground and glide into the valley that rippled below them gathering dust towers and anvil-head clouds that shot up to the cone of Mount Shasta. And so they entered California.

Then they entered a kind of whiteout, disappearing in heatwaves wobbling like mercury, horizon obscured by dust-haze, driving into it as if into a blizzard. Hour on hour the road was nothing more than the motion of the vehicle, would not have existed were it not for the vehicle, and no town nor any other fragments or outposts of civilization appeared in that netherworld of whiteness, a sere and blear-bleak zone of heat. No other cars either for a while, wind funneling in through the open windows. Gabriel's mouth was dry, and the scent of battery acid floated up from under the seat, sharp-tasting as it settled in the tissues of his mouth and nose. Occasional sleep tendrils drew him down into a shuddering waiting room, but there were no more attending dreams. Only heat and drowse and listless dropping away of body as he swooned and drifted and rose through the top of his head into the white-hot sky.

The names appeared on the green sign boards over the highway: Red Bluff, Corning, Orland, Willows, Arbuck, Dunning, Woodland, and out of that oblivion of dust came more cloverleaf offramps and more roadside diners and baseball fields and dancing affable inflatable hallelujah clowns summoning one and all to the dealerships. Then, another tree, first in a while. A few scanning crows clutching to a powerline. Vacaville and groves of trees with brittle scintillating leaves. And on into the low sun and flutter of late afternoon shadows as they pulled onto another highway out of Vallejo and onward as it all grew and densified with more cars and more warehouses and more cranes and construction sites, the defunct refineries of Richmond, the long-arcing erector set of the San Rafael bridge, the stuttering of guard rails and the shine of an estuary and the dip and bend of roads like Catherine wheels spinning them into their new lives.

At last they arrived in Berkeley.

The sun was fading, and their mother hunched over the steering wheel, exhausted, as they spun round and headed east off the freeway, driving up University Avenue to Oxford Street, left on Oxford, right on Hearst, left on Arch Street and up and then down to Virginia Street, the address, 1717, a little stucco triplex on the corner.

The first thing Gabriel noticed was the smell. It was not a bad smell but a strange smell, a smell of age, of the lives that inhabited these rooms and their accumulation pressed into a sort of wet shoe, tile and dirt and window-grime smell. The lower floor of their apartment had a living room and a small dining space and a kitchen. The upper floor had two bedrooms and a bathroom. The back stairway was narrow and dark, the steps covered with non-slip black strips of linoleum that curled at the edges. The place was furnished with a couch and table and bookshelves in the living room, a table and four chairs for eating in the kitchen. The bedrooms had saggy beds and desks like you'd find in school with shelves built into the sides. Nothing matched. Cooking pans looked hammered out by hand. Walls had a sticky orange sheen. Surfaces had gouges and ring stains. But most of all the place was crowded with an odor of ghosts.

Well, their mother said, this isn't so bad.

No, it's okay, Gabriel said, then he looked at his sister.

Yeah, she said and rolled her eyes and glanced around with the narrow scan she used on foul things entering her orbit.

You two decide which rooms you want upstairs, and no fighting about it. I'm way too tired to deal with that right now.

We won't, his sister said.

Where are you going to sleep? Gabriel asked.

I'll just use the fold out bed in the couch down here for now. Maybe I'll get a futon.

Shall we? his sister said, looking at him, and she lifted one eyebrow.

Okay.

They went upstairs and looked in the first room. Gabriel decided not to make a claim. He would let his sister choose. They looked in the second room. There was little difference between them. Then they went back to the first one. I'll take this one, she said.

All right. I'll take the other.

And so he went into his new room. The smell was all he could think about. He opened the window and caught the scent of something sweet and something else sort of minty and sharp wafting in, but it was still the smell of lives he noticed, that he seemed to sit inside like a passenger on a crowded bus. He turned on the light with a push-button switch, and it came on overhead, bright and stark for an interrogation. The room looked cold but felt hot. It looked empty even though it had furniture, and it felt crowded, even though he was alone.

Fall was already in the air, but it was different. It was hotter, drier with a few thin clouds cruising along with silver red vapor trails. He stood across the street from the new apartment. This was the spot his mother said to stand and wait. He wasn't alone. Another girl was there. She said her name was Anne. Eucalyptus trees, that's what they were called, she said. She lived across the street and knew what she was doing. The eucalyptus trees hung down like shaggy monsters with gray papery bark. The smells were complicated and new. Her apartment had three garage doors with half-moons carved into them. Occasional cars came down the hill, but otherwise Virginia Street was quiet beneath a double row of live oak trees; that's what she called them, live oaks. It was a strange name.

A man came up the street. He had long hair flying out from beneath a red bandana. He was leading a group of children. They were all holding hands, and they were all wearing helmets. Some of them were making strange grunts and growls. Some didn't appear to be looking where they were going. They were coming towards him, but before they reached the spot where he stood, the bus arrived, the door swung open, and he looked up into the bus at a large woman with a broad shiny dark face. She neither smiled nor spoke, just held the handle on the swing arm of the door and waited for him to get on.

He took an empty seat. There were four other children including the new girls. None of them sat together. They looked, in fact, as if they had chosen spots to keep them as far from each other as possible. Gabriel fit himself into the stand-off geometry. The bus lurched forward and he reached up to hold onto the seat back in front of him. It had a green rubber casing that had been picked at by the fingers of countless riders, and in one place someone had picked out chunks leaving a line of holes in the shapes of letters that spelled out the words FUCK YOU.

They rode down Virginia and stopped to pick up children every couple of blocks. No one sat together. They continued down and gradually the neighborhood changed. They passed liquor stores and vacant lots and a soup kitchen where a row of people stood in line against a wall. Cop cars slid by. Tents lined the sidewalks cluttered with shopping carts and garbage bags. One man leaned into the street and shook his fist and railed and ranted and otherwise scathed people who passed, and as the bus went by he looked up and for a moment he locked eyes with Gabriel and sent at him a searing missile of rage. Then a few blocks later they passed a man with orange gloves and a smile big as god waving at the passing cars.

The last stop was at a little house with a dirt yard worn smooth as cement, and there a kid with dirty jeans and a dirty shirt swung down from the limb of a tree and landed in the dirt and ran over to the bus. Gabriel heard someone behind him say, Arl's got rickets.

He turned and looked at the boy who had said it. What's rickets? he asked.

It makes your bones weak. You get it from eating dirt.

The boy got on board, and Gabriel saw that in fact he had no socks and that the skin of his arms and ankles was flaky with dirt.

When they arrived at the school, the playground was a mass of chaos. At one corner of the playground was a small building with a large smokestack. Beside it was a row of dumpsters, and from the smokestack black gouts of smoke were chugging into the air. Seagulls circled overhead in and out of the blocks of smoke.

Gabriel went into the office and stood in line to get his room assignment. A bell rang, and the hallway outside became an ambush of children. An old woman with shivering hands gave him a slip of paper with his name and the name of a teacher and a room number on it. He went down the hall, looking up at the room numbers until he came to the one that was his. He sat in the back towards the side, but not in the last row. Twitchy kids around him, zipping up back packs, rapping knuckles on the desk, carving initials into the wood. Another boy was eating a cheese stick and grinning. The teacher called the roll. When she got to his name she said, Thomas Bear? In previous grades he corrected his teachers and told them he went by his middle name. But something happened. He raised his hand and said, Here. Right away he thought someone would correct him but nobody noticed. And so he became someone else.

THE PRISONER'S DILEMMA

When he entered the showroom, it was like a carnival. Lights everywhere, cameras, news people interviewing the crowds and the players. People stood around in the glare of light flooding through the high showroom windows. Light. Too much light. And Jones forded the waves and clusters, people laughing garishly, people stretching and hydrating, getting themselves ready to become contestants. He held no ill feeling towards any of them. They were simply people, like him, trying for something, trying to win something for...the thing? Not just the thing, but to win. Sign Up Here, words on a banner, and beneath the banner a table and another cluster of people. He made his way towards it, saying, All right, the only words turning like a prayer in his mind while he was patting his pockets, all manner of thing. All right.

He stood in line. He looked around. So many people. It was like a party. He stepped forward in little paces. Once he reached the table, a young woman looked up at him as if surprised. She was rushing everyone through with a big smile and electric enthusiasm. She was impeccably arrayed in violet suit with diamond gecko stickpin at the throat and hair like a blue iron mane. Hello, she said.

Hello yourself.

You just sign in here, she said and handed him a clipboard. And when you're finished, I'll take that.

He sat in a little plastic chair at the edge of the table and filled out a questionnaire, blurry questions on a sheet of paper, questions about his health, his income, family background, and a final statement absolving the dealership of all responsibility if he should suffer any mishap, injury, physical or psychological harm in the process of the contest. He signed it and turned it in.

Very good, she said and smiled and took his sheet of paper and laid it on a stack of other papers and handed him a sticker upon which he was to write his name below a greeting that said Hello My Name Is...

Good luck!

Thank you very much!

One last trip to the bathroom, through the crowds, faces in the mirrors, hands slicking back hair, hands washing faces. In the stall he downed several mini bottles one after another. Ah, fortified. Sounds around him like a busy shipyard. And replenished, he emerged with the benevolent glow of the freshly anointed, the baptized, the graced. He slapped his sides and waded out into the showroom. He smiled into the crowd. Let us begin.

Approaching the group clustered around the vehicle, he was handed a pair of white gloves, and with pontiff aplomb he put them on. For the laying on of hands, he said aloud to no one in particular. Are we, after all, handling a holy relic? But no one really heard him, at least that was what he thought as he stepped between the shoulders of two other people and slipped his gloved hand onto the left rear quarter panel of the prize.

The crowd was thick and jostling, but he pressed his hand firmly to his chosen spot as if win or lose he would defend it to the last and hold. Lay on...he said. People around him talked and laughed. The camera crews moved in. Then the Dealer came over and lifted his arms as if delivering a homily. He wore a bright white shirt and gray slacks, and his hair was black crisp and combed back tight over the top of his head. He had strong white teeth that gleamed. The cameras turned to him, and he spoke:

Good morning everyone. Good to have you here! I'm Don Anderson, owner and manager, and it is with great pleasure that I welcome you all to Anderson's Dealership and to our seventh annual giveaway contest! He paused, nodding, and the crowd cheered. The lights of the camera crews intensified the whiteness of his face. As you know, each year we've done this we've started off with quite a crowd, and this year seems to be no exception. Families and friends are of course welcome to stay throughout the competition. We only ask that in your support you conduct yourselves with courtesy and respect to all the contestants. All right? Now, let us review some of the basic rules. First of all, contestants must keep one hand on the vehicle at all times. Accidentally releasing your hold will result in immediate dismissal. In fact, if for any reason your hand should come off, you will be dismissed from the competition. There are no exceptions. We will have fifteen-minute breaks every three hours, and as you can see we have food available at the sign-in table, but contestants must be back at their places promptly at the end of the breaks or they will be disqualified. Any physical contact, pushing or harassment of other contestants will result in disqualification. If any support members harass or physically contact other contestants, the contestant they are associated with will be disqualified. There will be no exceptions to any of these rules. The contest will continue until there is only one person left. The last contestant who remains in contact wins. This is a promotional event, and no members of the dealership, their families or friends are eligible. Are there any questions? He waited a moment, during which the crowd twittered and muttered.

Someone then shouted out, What about a glamper van?

They can start their own contest! he shot back, grinning broadly. Now, let the contest begin, and good luck to all of you!

The camera crews moved in closer to interview Don Anderson, and he soaked up the light and the attention and puffed up like an octopus in an ink cloud. Then the news crews went around the car and zeroed in on various contestants, asking them their names and their occupations and their strategies for success. When they reached Jones with their battery of lights and camera lenses, the young reporter in his sharp sport coat punched the microphone forward although his eyes remained quick-scanning. Jones squirmed while facing them squarely and keeping his hand firmly on the panel. And he said, Yes, it's a bit awkward here, can't you tell, but it's all really a test of fortitude, isn't it? The machine is symbolic, mostly, the goal itself an abstract reason for the attempt, and the game which finds each of us here is to test the mettle! The game is the field wherein each one of us must search out that inner reservoir of strength, face our inner demons and so forth...but before he was finished, the crews moved on.

After a few more passes the camera crews left and gradually the crowd of onlookers diminished until the only people who remained were either the workers or families and friends of the contestants or the odd few people who had actually come to shop. The first few hours after that were like a boat trip in which the contestants more or less got acquainted.

Here we are! Someone said, and they all laughed.

Yes indeed. We're the chosen few.

Not so few, yet.

Rather like Noah's ark, don't you think?

Except without the pairs.

I heard that last year it went for three days.

Three days!

The hardest part is when you have to go to the bathroom.

Thank God for the breaks!

Just hope they come when you need them!

And the primary recurring joke with smile and raised eyebrows was, who would be the first to fall away?

The afternoon faded and they settled into a pattern of chatting and silent staring. Some struck up friendships and agreed that they had to get together after this was all through. Some attended only to their friends and families. Everyone was friendly, and everyone was having a good time. Jones kept up a more or less unbroken monologue, the contents of which were the more obscure benefits of the contest such as this chance meeting over a more or less hallowed possession made hallowed by a devotion which itself is quite meaningless since being here and staying here is an existential quandary so that what we're here to face, the ultimate abstraction ensconced in physical mortification may be different for everyone, regardless of the so-called prize.

Then why don't you step away and just visit? someone said.

Yeah, make no mistake, this competition has a very real goal.

Who isn't in it for the vehicle?

Wait, so, if the vehicle is meaningless, or if we're supposed to believe it's meaningless as you're trying to convince us, then losing is…what, a weakness of character? Is that what you mean?

That's it! That's it in a nutshell!

You're just trying to talk us into letting go!

Ah, you sense the subtle prevarication of my argument, Jones said.

Everything you say has another meaning.

The meaning of all oration is persuasion.

Didn't I read that once in a fortune cookie?

Perhaps I just mean for myself.

That's right, you're talking to yourself.

Yeah, that's right! You're all alone here. No one else exists!

Laughter.

Ah, but you do, Jones said. And soon I shall address you all by name. But what I mean by the vehicle not existing is that we cannot become attached to its qualities that put us into the chain of cause and effect. You see, if you really listen, I am giving you clues on how to win. Qualities and change have their origin in nature. The vehicle is abstract at best. Finger pointing at the moon and all, you see? What I'm saying is that if you see the car as the object of your desire, if you set it off in value from other things it becomes a trap, but if you see it through the discipline of one who sees the whole charade with clarity, you will be master of the field!

Okay, preacher.

Yeah, what are *you* selling?

I represent no official denominations, corporations, institutions....

Then what's your message?

The three dogs of hell that destroy the self are desire, anger and greed.

Then what are you doing here?

Training the mind. This is an opportunity to practice discipline. As long as one is focused on the act without craving the fruit, then one remains free of all pain and illusion.

And disappointment, preacher?

Absolutely, to say the least.

So why not step away?

To step away would be a failure in engagement; relinquishing without resolution leads to dark inertia.

You're going to feel some dark inertia all right.

Lucid. The object here is to remain lucid. That is what I'm here for.

I'm here for the vehicle. That's lucid enough for me.

Good luck, preacher.

And to you.

And they passed into the evening with no one dropping away. On breaks, they stretched and went to the bathroom and ate from the complimentary food buffet provided by the dealership. Jones replenished himself in secret, but he already knew his supply wouldn't last long, and so his mind worked on a plan for obtaining drink. But he conjured up nothing, which raised the specter of the possibility that he would in fact run out. And what horrors would that bring? Of course, he could just as easily walk away if the need became too great, and as he stood in the bathroom stall and pulled the last of his mini bottles from his pocket and drained its contents and left it up-ended in his mouth long past the thirteenth drop to fully draw in its vapor, the thought of quitting both comforted and despaired him. Yes, he could walk away, that was true, but only if the need were too great. But to walk away simply from a need for drink? What kind of admission was that? And what was it he was really after? A vehicle? The great wheel? Ironic as his statements were about the fruits and the goal of remaining lucid, he was not altogether immune to such an attraction, even if it had only occurred to him on the spot as a kind of joke.

Thus the trial commenced. And it began in the legs, the ache in the calves and the chalky grinding in the knees. He stepped from foot to foot in order to keep the circulation going, but he felt his muscles beginning to cramp, then brief and unsettling moments of numbness. The calves and thighs rippled with fiery tingles. The hip joints rocked in angry opposition, and he had no way to escape from the intense awareness of his reticulated bones and accordion flesh. Sharp pains flared up, spikes of weird electric fire leaped through his thighs and up his spine, and he seethed inwardly and breathed fiercely. Even the air seemed to singe as though his nerves were exposed in a horrible whole-body root canal.

And as the effect of the alcohol began to drain away, he felt the first finger-weight of an enormous weariness. An overwhelming desire to lie down, to sleep. His eyes closed for long periods until he lost balance and jerked awake and clung more tightly with his gloved hand to the edge of the quarter panel. Glancing around, he saw that some of the others had also closed their eyes, trying for little shots of sleep while standing. One man at the taillight stood staring with a poker grin, an edge of the fire Dobbs smiling and waiting for people to drift off and let go the treasure. The game began to change.

The first to drop away was a young woman at the fender who simply shook her head and smiled and stepped away, peeling the glove from her hand. The group noticed and everyone awakened and turned towards her, and the general sentiment was an initial shock and brief disappointment, then a wave of consolation and at last a spark of predatory glee as they came together in a sudden cheer. The woman smiled and waved and said, I'm going to go have a good night's sleep. See you all! And as she walked away, they all felt the exhilaration of lasting past the first person quitting and coming that much closer to winning.

In the early morning hours before dawn, Jones began to pass through the firewaves of the coming hangover. He saw family and friends of the other contestants sitting nearby or sleeping on the floor around them, and in the red waves of his mind they were circling sharks. His eyes burned. He drank water on the breaks, but he remained as parched as someone who drinks from the sea. His nose began to run and his head reeled with white hot pain that burned behind his eyes. Nausea persisted, and on breaks he sometimes vomited.

You'd better give in, preacher, Dobbs said. That was the name by which Jones now considered him. He was a small, wiry man with a stubble of beard. He wore a green plaid shirt rolled up at the sleeves, forearms tattooed with mermaid and cross and crown of thorns, and in his breast pocket was a little device with a wire winding up to an earphone in his ear.

Quite all right, Jones said. I am only freeing myself from delusions.

You think that pain in your legs is a delusion?

Quite. It's not so bad, now.

Well, you know, I'm sad for you because that's really a bad sign. That means your legs are dying, your blood is pooling in your veins and you're more and more susceptible to clotting. That's really dangerous. You know that?

Are you saying your legs don't hurt?

They do, but I haven't been drinking like you have. I've been in training for this. I'm healthy. I'm strong. Look at you. You look like you're dying.

Another delusion.

That's a bad sign, too, that way you're thinking. Now you don't even see what kind of danger you're in. I feel sorry for you.

I appreciate your concern.

The man smiled with bare tooth malice. Jones closed his eyes and floated in the void, losing the feeling of his legs and his hand on the car, his body entire, and he did not spring back, not this time, but traveled forward over mind and memory and saw and dove into a child like a creature crawling through the dead of night and opening a door to the feminine breathing of sky as he was swept up in a swirl of stars towards a pale lightwave cowling in cobra flare, mother source of all and the opening from which came.

Others drifted away during the night, but he was not aware of their departure, and as the light came through the showroom windows he counted and saw that now only twelve remained, including himself. A boy of about eighteen was standing on his left, and his mother stood to his right. His father was nearby too. Jones nodded to each of them and said, Good morning. Dobbs stood fierce at the rear left taillight, a complacent squint to his face as if he were posted there to adjust the levels of their pain. Jones turned to the boy's mother and said, Increasing the chances by coming as a group, eh?

She smiled. She was a petite woman with epicanthic fold over eyes barely open with fatigue. She stood with her shoulders hunched in the posture of defeat. I'm not sure how much it will increase our chances being together, she said, and I'm not sure how much longer I want to stay with it. We mostly want to win it for our son, Carl.

Oh, do stay. You're doing fine. You've made it this far. Surely you can make it a little longer.

Yeah, Mom. You can do it.

Carl retained the bright demeanor of youth for whom it was still an amusing game.

And from where do you hail? Jones asked.

Here! The boy said. I'm a student at the university.

Tremendous! And what are you studying there?

Environmental engineering.

Most noble. Most noble. We need your help, I'm afraid. Any specialties?

Urban design, mostly. Although, lately I've been pretty fascinated by the possibilities of bioremediation.

Bioremediation?

It's a way to use naturally occurring enzymes and organisms for environmental clean-up, which in combination with good urban engineering can help to stabilize some of our environmental problems.

I have more hope just standing next to you. You'll save the world one day, I'm sure of it, if my generation doesn't foolishly try to interfere.

They're the ones giving me my grades.

I'll put in a good word.

Supporting friends and family rose and gathered up sleeping bags from the floor, and now they were all back to a sense of support and community fun. Some news crews had returned and were interviewing people. The general commentary focused on hope and what winning would mean and complaints about fatigue, especially in the back and legs.

As the sunlight intensified, so too did the heat, and in his bleary-minded, hungover and sleep-deprived state, Jones felt his body wavering in a woolly kind of dissipation, as though the borders of his form were giving way to the morass of warm air, and he watched through long, trance-like moments as time seemed to slow down and move in tedious incremental muffled clangs, as though the escapement of the grand clock of the world were mired in sand. The people around him moved more slowly and froze in brief moments becoming motionless cutouts of themselves. Two boys stood opposite each other on the other side of the room tossing a baseball back and forth, and as Jones watched he saw the baseball's line of trajectory punctuated with infinite after-images like ellipses dotting the air with one succeeding the other from hand to hand.

Now more he felt the urge to sleep. After the afternoon break, he saw that several people did not return, including the mother who had stood beside him. And while Carl didn't appear disappointed, he, too, now had a vacant gaze and seemed to drift from himself, as did many of the others, several of whom could no longer keep their eyes open. Only Dobbs at the tail light seemed implacable, immovable, almost malevolent in his obstinate enjoyment of their suffering, particularly that of Jones whom he seemed to fixate on with unrelenting stare.

The fatigue of standing in one spot becomes ludicrous. Pain comes in waves. Why choose to do this to yourself? To choose this pain for material wealth, to choose this pain when others suffer for no reason at all? It seemed an insult to true misfortune. There is in this some moral desuetude. Pain rolls in waves. It settles in places, lodges like a spider weaving its necrotic threads. To move is not to dislodge the pain but to open breaks in its general fabric which then fill in from other strained sources to radiate even more. The only way to deal with this is to take oneself out of the body. The only way of taking oneself out of the body is to let go. Letting go is like that first dive from the tower, the first moment looking down at the black water below and the little waves rolling in. What will it be like, striking that water? Something is moving. Light breaks through a cloud. Crows are watching. I love the grace of the gull coming in from the sea. Looking down he watched his hand sink through the metal fabric of the vehicle.

She appeared like the queen in a three-card monte game. A few faces shuffled, a few hands reached in for drinks, money hit the counter, and there she was. He waited for his drink. Where was his drink? He put in his order, didn't he? So where was it? He wanted to complain, but he didn't want to make a scene. She was all black hair and black lips and stone coal black eyes. Her skin was Egyptian sacrament. Her movements were animated by wind, hope, pure improvised grace. He watched her, and she watched him. No one around them interrupted. There was a crowd and noise and yet her proximity and coolness were enough to convince him that they were there alone together.

Still worried? she said and smiled.

He smiled in return, aligned his expression to hers. I'm reminded of the man who kept a Gideon Bible in his bedside drawer to maintain the sensation of living in motels.

Every move is everlasting.

When in California…?

She laughed. Loss is the hardest real estate to sell.

That's true, that's true, and when I left those things behind in the last apartment, I thought I needed them. When we moved into the garage of…what was their name? It escapes me, now, but I do remember the son was institutionalized. For a brief period they let me have his room, as long as I didn't disturb anything. Line drawings all over the place, self-portraits with a kind of electric energy in the ink, the energy of madness I thought would infect me if I stayed there too long. The things. I thought I needed them. I really did. But after a while, I couldn't even remember what I'd left behind.

And the hat?

Slouch hat? Top hat?

The hat on the billboard.

Oh, the recurring hat. I never got that one.

No?

No, I never did, but I kept seeing it everywhere.

Try again.

How?

Try. Free associate.

Hmmm. All right. Hat rat cat…head…top of the head… consciousness…hat…hats…jobs…selves…identities…I still don't get it.

She laughed again. It's a joke.

You could drive a truck through the vaults of my ignorance. What is?

Hats.

I don't get it! He smiled lamely.

In a strong wind?

What?

Picture it.

A strong wind. The hat blows off. I go chasing after it…

She laughed. You still don't get it?

He smiled. Well, I think I do.

No you don't.

The problem is how to live without feeling trapped in your own skin. Books are not enough, buying time on quick Sunday, smoking the clock, crawling through these moments going slow as a slow breath out and see, time moves aligned to inhale and exhale, hold as long as you can to the indelible dream of air.

And as she moved in closer to him perhaps to give him a kiss, and he felt himself falling back, back, falling.

Night. Only nine remained. Carl had left, but the father remained. Dobbs stood smiling at the taillight. A man at the hood didn't look well. He was older, bowed forward with his arms crossed on the hood. A friend or relative stood beside him, rubbing his back and whispering into his ear. Occasionally he lifted his head and on his face was a look of such agony it was painful to see. Those near him turned away. Only Jones and Dobbs unflinching looked on. Jones felt locked in gaze, felt the ache, nausea, torpor, the desire to relinquish. Relinquish. The word itself was like a twin blade. One edge cut desire for self and desire to let go, while the other edge cut away the man who appeared in such distress that Jones in his twilight state believed him close to death, believed as he watched that the friend at the man's side was not friend as he appeared but succubus with puckered mouth and tentacle arms and suckers on the fingertips that siphoned life energy rising like a vapor from the older man's shoulders and head. Relinquish and stand down! Save yourself! The older man looked up. Tears were in his eyes, and then as if he'd been given permission he lifted his hand and stepped away from the vehicle and the succubus switched back to friend and led him carefully away.

Well done, Dobbs said. Well done. Now you're learning.

What happened to the support, preacher? the father asked.

What? Jones looked at Dobbs, the father, realizing maybe he had spoken aloud.

Yeah, a woman said. She stood at the headlight. That was pretty opportunistic of you.

The man was obviously suffering.

We're all suffering, the father said.

Lighten up, Dobbs said. He saw a weakness and he took a shot. It was the right move. May have even saved the guy's life, for all you know.

Jones closed his eyes and stood on the tower as the water moved below, light constellating over its surface. Let go. How would it feel to enter the dark river? That first strike? What would wearing that name be like? He took a step forward, hands poised above his head, and dove. The air for a moment was cool shudder, then he hit the water, and as if someone slapped the top of his head he heard and felt a crack as he sank into darkness. Once in the water his limbs loosened and he felt the force of momentum slow and suspend and stop. Nothing moved. Then he turned towards light coming from above and splayed out like the spindle fibers of creation flowing down and dividing around him. He lingered in the dark water drifting with his breath abeyed and all thought blown out.

I'm the devil, you know, Dobbs said. And you're going straight to hell. You know that, don't you? I'm here, at this crossroads, to help you. Did you know that? I've been here all along, even before you knew it. In fact it was my idea for you to come down here. I've been listening to your thoughts. I've given you half of them, tuned your mind for this and every moment like this. You can't lose, now. Look at these people. They don't have your grit. They're dying off. But not you. You're feeling good, aren't you? You have to admit it, and you haven't had a drink in…how long now? How long has it been? What do you think you should be feeling like right about now? Under normal circumstances? What would you feel like any other time going this long without a drink? Think about it. You don't have any explanation for it, for how good you feel. You could go for three more days. More than that! How many days has it been? How many nights? You can't even remember, can you? That's because I took you out of time. It can't touch you. You could stand here forever. Look at these people. Look at them. That guy there, he better give in because he's surely going to have a heart attack if he doesn't. Why don't you give him a little nudge, a little healthy advice? I think he needs it right about now. He would listen to you at this point. Just tell him to slip away. And look at that poor father. He wants it for his son, but he doesn't have more than a few hours before he passes out. Look how hard he's breathing. That's it, don't you know? Just the three of you. You're all that's left. Amazing, isn't it? You didn't notice the others had left already. Now it's just the three of you, and you're the clear winner. Isn't it obvious? Just look at you. And you owe it all to me. There can't be any doubt about that in your mind. Not now. Just look at how good you feel.

It's not you, Jones said.

No? Dobbs smiled. Can you be sure? Are you willing to take that risk? To risk your soul?

Then the mother appeared before him, face drawn tight. Why don't you give up? She was crying, her face full of empirical righteousness. You're killing him. Just stop it. Stop this right now! And then she was gone.

He closed his eyes.

Look at me. I'm as helpless as a kitten up a tree, not knowing my right foot from my left, my hat from my gloves. I'm too misty and too much...

Where was his drink? He slid his hands across the surface of the piano. How long ago had he ordered his drink? Why wasn't it here? A couple across from him sat with their heads together. They had drinks. Why didn't he have his drink? Hands passed over his eyes. A flutter of wings. A few faces appeared and then were gone. The piano singer looked up from the bottom of a hole formed by the surface of the piano and all its reflections scrolled into a funnel. Jones looked up at a point of light far above. He willed himself towards it. But he didn't move. He willed again and this time felt himself rising, but when he relaxed his will he slipped back and the light retreated a reluctant distance behind the exit sign. He felt anxiety and a beating like bat wings somewhere behind his eyes. Some learning, some lessons asserted themselves. He concentrated on letting go of the anxiety and this gave him buoyancy. He was floating upwards, or maybe the light was telescoping down, but as he approached it he became self-conscious and fell back into his spot again with no drink in sight. Where was his drink? He gathered the will once again to fend off all thought other than that light, and he rose, approached, broke through into—

Just you and me, buddy. Dawn was coming through the showroom window. The others had all left. And for the moment, Jones and

Dobbs were alone. He stood facing the man with an odd feeling of compassion. Then Dobbs smiled and said, You remember what I told you? I'm taking you to your peak. I'm taking you to that point where you don't think you can go any farther, then I'm going to step away, and when I do, you'll have your reward and I'll have your soul. Look at that thing. It sure is beautiful, isn't it?

The news crews returned, and they asked how the last two contestants were doing. Dobbs said, I think we're both feeling pretty good. We might go a couple more days. Dobbs never blinked nor took his eyes off Jones.

The dealer arrived and circled the two men and said, Well, well, we're at the final showdown, I see. The last stand-off. Let's see if we can't make this a dramatic finale, eh boys?

You should be feeling pain right now, Dobbs said to Jones. Why aren't you? You ask yourself that? Why aren't you feeling any pain?

Time moved in slow blur moments, and people and images shuddered in and out of focus, moving on the periphery but gone when he turned his head to see. Vultures fluttered at the windows. Jackals moved in the shadows near the showroom doors, and the floor rippled like reptile flesh, rising and falling, rising and falling, and little blue energy waves rolled out from his chest as he breathed.

Why aren't you feeling anything?

A boy with a baseball cap approached from outside, and as the automatic doors opened a breeze knocked his hat from his head and he jumped and chased after it.

It's a joke, get it?

Light glittered along the surface of all the new vehicles in the showroom. Light gleamed along the tight fabric of his gloved hand. Light emanated from the bodies of the people around him.

I'm taking you to your peak. I'm tuning your mind.

Wax world melting slowly, slowly grinding down, coming to a stop. Dobbs stepped back, smiling as he backed away, and it was as if he simply vanished into thin air and was gone. Jones was alone, the last one standing at the vehicle, claiming it with his touch.

And we have a winner! the dealer shouted. Our winner, folks!

The news crews gathered around in a tight circle, their cameras in his face, their lights blinding. How do you feel? How did you do it? What are you going to do now?

We have our winner, the dealer shouted, and he grabbed Jones's wrist and lifted his arm into the air. Congratulations to our winner!

And as if awakening, Jones looked out through the shell of his skull and the tunnel of his eyes at the strange circus swirling around him.

PART FOUR

THE ZERO-SUM GAME

Arl's job was to hold the beggar's sign and stand at the freeway exit where the cars came to a stop at the light. He and the others worked in three-hour shifts and any money they got they brought back to the rest of the crew in the camp under the overpass. The sign was a piece of cardboard with the words in black marking pen:

Homeless
Anything will help
Even a Smile
God Bless

Sometimes people did smile, sometimes they gave him change, mostly they just ignored him. One woman rolled down her window and spat on him. Four boys in a dark sedan opened their windows and howled and swerved to hit him, coming so close the gravel sprayed against his legs as he stumbled back to get out of the way. A man in a pickup truck threw pennies at his feet with a vicious sneer, and Arl wondered why people would bother to give anything at all if they despised the giving so much, so Arl just smiled in return and bent and picked up the money.

His legs turned to pins and needles. Rain no longer bothered him. Cars went by in a blur. Faces began to look the same, staring ahead, eyes fixed into the distance as though the oblivious gaze were the universal mind expressing itself in multitude with only a rare kind of consciousness even aware of Arl's presence. When his shift was up, he folded the sign beneath his arm and headed back to the camp.

He kicked through the loose gravel street past the convenience store and the abandoned cafe made to look like the Leaning Tower of Pisa. Planes overhead swept down through the broken clouds and aligned their flight paths to the airport. Arl climbed through the open flap of wire fence and crossed the muddy field that used to be a schoolyard. He climbed the track-worn path up the hill through the ivy and dropped down into camp. T was there with a little campfire going. He glanced up when he saw Arl and grinned a brief grin over teeth that looked like a mouthful of coal. Jones was asleep and wrapped in a rug. And Michelle sat leaned against the cement stanchion and seemed not yet to notice him, her eyes narrow and staring into the fire.

Hey there, cowboy. How'd you fare? T asked.

Nickels and dimes'll do ya, Arl said. He crouched down near the fire and put his hands out and felt the warmth on his palms.

Safe and sound, good to see, T said, speaking more out of the side of his mouth than directly, keeping his face at an angle as though he were constantly turning away.

We'll eat good tonight, Arl said. After a few more rounds at the entrance we should pick up enough coin by dark.

Arl glanced over at Michelle who still didn't move, didn't glance back or even show yet that she noticed him. He looked at T who gazed hard into the fire, then he looked back at Michelle and said, You okay? She didn't respond, so he leaned over and laid the inside of his forearm against her cheek and pulled it back quick and said, Shew, honey, you're burnin' up. Have you had anything to eat today?

She tilted her head just enough to line him up in her vision, and though he couldn't see her mouth move he heard her say, slowly and quietly as if whispering a secret, I'm not hungry.

Shoot, honey. You got to eat, he said. But she just leaned her head back against the cement and more or less looked into the fire, her eyes barely open if in fact she was looking at anything at all.

T, we got any soup?

Nope.

How long she been like this?

Since she got up, I guess. I haven't really paid her much attention though, she's been so quiet. I had to go out on a little mission of my own this morning, too.

What kind of mission?

Just trying to scare up some scratch, same as you.

Man, we've got to keep an eye on the camp. And did you get anything?

The world hasn't been very generous today.

You were out begging drugs.

No siree I was not.

And you left her here like this?

I told you, I didn't see that she was having any trouble. She just seemed a bit pensive today.

Pensive? Dammit T, she's burning up with fever.

And I'm supposed to know that?

We're supposed to be looking out for each other.

I do! I look out for all of us. And if I had been beggin' for drugs, which I wasn't, wouldn't that have been just the thing? Seems to me all she needs is a little pinch and she'd be just all right.

What she needs is food. What have we got around here?

Well, we're fresh out of everything as it turns out. I'm not trying to be smart. That's just a plain fact.

You got any money?

No I do not.

What about Jones?

I can't speak for him.

Arl rose from his spot by the fire and leaned down over Jones in the rug. He listened and had he not known better he would have thought the man was dead, but motionless and silent as the body in the rug was he knew that Jones was deep in drinker's oblivion. Without much confidence he nudged the sleeping man with his foot. Jones. Jonesy, wake up. He shoved at him harder with the heel of his boot, but there was just no rousing the man.

Ah, leave him alone. You know he ain't come back with anything but a hangover.

Then Arl heard Michelle speaking, but her voice was quieter than the howl of traffic above them that never let up, not by day and not in the thinnest hours of night— it kept up, a constant sound like wind preceding a storm which never arrives or more likely comes and keeps coming and never actually leaves. Arl leaned down and listened at her lips. Shhh, she was saying. And, Shhhh, as if trying to hush him or hush someone else nearby or something she heard only in her own mind.

Well, I'm going to go get her something to eat, some soup. That's what she needs. Arl stood up looking around the meager camp of cardboard boxes and filthy blankets and the pile of wood that each of them had contributed to by collecting from the broken remains of the school.

Pick us up a bottle, too, while you're at it, will ya?

Arl shook his head and bared his teeth and just about said something but didn't. Instead, he leaned back down and said into Michelle's ear, You just sit tight, honey. I'll be right back.

He went back down the little path and back through the school-yard and out to the street. The convenience store nearby was like an oasis in the otherwise abandoned neighborhood where they could pick up just about anything they needed, whatever was on the shelves: juice and soup, some bread and if they had enough money maybe a little meat. She probably wouldn't eat much, and most likely was suffering more from some withdrawal, but she would die without liquids. And if he could do anything to prevent that he would, regardless of what Jones might say should he awake some-time soon, which was unlikely, about how to spend their money. Because disproportionate as their sensibilities were regarding communal responsibility, Arl was clear on one thing—that the first and foremost concern was their collective survival. Nothing else mattered, not the desire for drunkenness and its peaceful if brief liber-ation from their geography of doom, nor any other kind of escape which was transitory and seemed to include with it returning with intensified awareness of the gloom and boredom of being nowhere.

He went up the street and into the convenience store. He nodded once to the clerk as if to say, yes I'm here and I acknowledge my state but I am in fact going to buy something not steal. The clerk was a thin Ichabod with a long neck and pimple face. He wore the synthetic green vest of clerks and squinted with a sour expression that said hurry up and get your stuff and get out of here.

Arl grabbed some chicken broth, a jug of orange juice, a loaf of Wonder bread and a package of sliced turkey. He went up to the counter and laid it all down and began to empty out his pockets. The clerk rang up the total. Arl pulled out handful after handful of coins. He counted them out and was exactly twelve cents short. He looked at the clerk. The clerk looked at him.

You got to put something back, the clerk said.

It's twelve cents.

You got to put something back.

What about your little penny jar, there, Arl said, pointing at a little tray with a hand written card taped to it that said, Take a Penny, Give a Penny. The clerk emptied the tray into his palm and counted them out. You're still three cents short.

Three cents?

A man pushed the front door open and leaned in but didn't enter entirely, and he said, You got a bathroom?

Sure, the clerk said, and he turned and pointed at a key attached to a spatula that hung on a hook at the end of the counter. The man came in and grabbed the key and went back out. The clerk stood there and looked at Arl and said, So what's it going to be?

You can't let three cents slide?

Look, that means I have to pay for it. You know how many people come in here and come up short? You know how much a day I'd be giving out if I gave everybody three cents?

I need this food, all of it.

Then go beg someone else for the three cents.

Arl looked around. There was the man in the bathroom. He could go ask him. The thought of it made his throat pulse. He started to go out, leaving the food on the counter. Then he stopped. Three cents, he said. Look, I got a friend who needs to eat. She's sick.

You got to put something back.

Arl picked up the food and started walking out of the store.

I wouldn't do that if I were you, buddy. The clerk didn't follow. Arl kept on walking without looking back.

Arl hiked back down the road. If the clerk called the cops which most likely he wouldn't, Arl would already be back at the camp. He probably wouldn't be able to go back to that store again, at least not while that particular clerk was there, but in time it would all pass from the mind and memory and then what would it matter? Unless they put up a wanted poster.

He took one look back before ducking under the wire fence. Nobody was following. Nobody was even around. He detoured past the remains of the school and picked up a few pieces of wood. It would be dark soon. Rain was coming down light and swirling from a gray sky mouth. The temperature dropped since he stood by the freeway, and it felt like night was going to be cold. They needed a fire and a good one.

Back in the camp no one had moved since he left. Jones was still sleeping under the rug and would probably stay there till morning. Michelle sat stone still, only now her eyes were closed. T crouched near the fire, but his eyes had the agitated light of an animal that wants be on the move. He worked his lips over his teeth and spat once into the fire and said, What'd ya get?

Food.

Ah, well, thanks for the provisions.

It won't last past tomorrow.

I didn't figure.

We need more money, Arl said, as he crouched by the fire and added some wood and arranged the meager provisions at his feet.

I suppose it's my turn to go stand by the freeway, T said.

You can't expect Michelle to do it.

I wasn't suggesting it, even if she hasn't gone in two days.

Look at her.

Probably get more money in her condition.

She's not going anywhere.

I wasn't saying so. T rose and took the sign and was on his way.

Hold on there, Arl said, and he slid a few pieces of meat between two slices of bread and handed it to T who took the sandwich and crammed half of it into his mouth before he even left the camp.

Arl opened the can of soup with a pocketknife and tilted the lid and set it on a stone at the edge of the fire. He checked Michelle. Her face looked drawn and tight and thin as a cadaver's skull. He reached and laid the back of his wrist against her brow and felt the heat burn through his shirtsleeve. Michelle. Michelle, he said, but her eyes didn't open. Her face was dull as an old coin. Even before this sickness she was beginning to fade. Some current was faltering that conducted the energy to sustain whatever it took to meet the world and behold and wonder as though she were slipping into a gone dream out of which she might peak in the twitch of sleep in the sleep of fever as the light dimmed into evening, as if she were returning from the brink of departing with a quick intake of breath, her eyes opening with something fierce.

On first meeting her there'd been a hint of romance between them, but a hidden story she wouldn't speak of prevented anything from developing. All he really knew was that she was afraid her father would find her, certain she would never escape him, that no matter where she went or what name she took or how she changed in appearance he would find her, and whatever life she created for herself or whatever unlikely family she might even dream of having, he would return to destroy everything. She tried charms. She tried rituals and ceremonies, but a psychic saw it in mysterious cards—the return of the father. It was fated to happen. There was nothing she could do to stop it.

The soup started to boil, and Arl pulled it away from the fire and stirred it with a spoon and set it aside to cool. Michelle, he said, but she didn't respond. He leaned in close and felt the heat of her fever against his face. Michelle!

The eyes opened slightly, gum-crusted along the rims. And a brief smile rose on her lips, the flicker of something there. Arl, she whispered.

I made you some soup, he said.

Ah, you sweetheart. She pulled herself up slowly, as though working heavy machinery. Ooh have I got the aches.

You've got to eat a little something.

I don't know.

Try.

I'll try.

He wrapped some cloth from a torn bed sheet around the tin can and lifted it to her. She reached out a hand to take it, but the hand shook so badly he held the can instead and dipped the spoon into the cup and brought it to her lips. She took little sips, actually ate some of the soup, and it made him feel better. At least he was doing something.

T here? she asked.

No.

Jones?

Here but unable to answer.

Where's T?

He's on duty.

It's my turn, isn't it?

Not tonight.

She seemed to perk up a bit and pulled her hand out from under the blanket and took the spoon and shakily dished up some mouthfuls. I should go out.

No you don't. I won't allow it.

Did you go?

I just got back a little while ago.

How'd you do?

Got this food. He spread his arms as if to reveal a feast.

She reached out and touched his cheek. Angel, she said. And she leaned forward as if to whisper something to him when someone stepped into the firelight, a figure more a piece of darkness sheared off and looking around. Who—she said, eyes more open, so that Arl turning to see what she saw only caught a vague outline and thought for a moment her father had returned as predicted. The chicken-necked clerk from the convenience store stood with his shadow stretched out longer than he was but thinner, if that were possible, and twitching like a black flame. He wore the same vest and sneer and said in a voice too loud, Here they are! And the absurdity of it, the motivation of three cents that would send this underpaid and undermined little man into the dark in search of a transient made Arl laugh a little, until he saw that the man had brought others with him.

They came into the camp and before Arl could even count them they kicked at the fire and kicked at Arl. They went after Michelle and Jones in his rug. Arms swept down and then sticks and more kicks and it all came in such a fury that there was no chance for Arl or Michelle to respond except for lighting their hands. Every attempt to rise was met with a flurry of vicious blows as if the very effort to rise inspired more attacks. Then Arl heard laughter of a sick kind and saw only through the blur of arms and legs and sweep of smoke the shadows dragging Michelle out to the edge of the camp where others descended like night vultures upon her. He may have shouted but then a blow came to his stomach and stole all sound and breath. Then another blow came to his head, and the scene and the night and every thought went black.

When Arl came around he heard T shouting, What the hell? Arl! What the hell? But the voice came from a distance, as though T were speaking from a sewer well. Then Arl saw the flux of shadows and a face locked on him with eyes that stared into his eyes and skin slick as snake flesh. Then another blow came and he was gone.

When Arl came around again, he was lying next to the cement pillar. Michelle lay nearby. Jones was up from his rug and gone. T was hunched at the burned-out fire, his bloody face and bloody chin resting on his bloody knees, but his eyes were open and staring.

T? Arl said.

Yeah. T did not look up.

You all right?

I'm all right. You all right?

Think so. He felt nauseous. His legs and his arms and his stomach and his chest all cramped with pain. Moving felt like it was breaking things internally. His head throbbed. His mouth tasted of blood and as he rose and opened his mouth he felt the crackle of dry blood on his scalp and face. Jesus, he said.

You look like him right about now.

Arl looked down at Michelle. Her clothes were torn and bloody beneath the green wool of her coat. He leaned down and said to her, Michelle, you okay?

She groaned a sound that meant she was but didn't want to talk. Arl looked around. There was the empty can of soup. The bread had been stomped into the dirt. The meat lay in the ashes of the fire.

We're going to have to move from here, T said.

Arl said nothing and closed his eyes.

The three of them walked across the schoolyard and down the road away from the store and away from the freeway entrance that had provided access to a stream of money for three months. They walked past burned-out apartments and abandoned warehouses and rows of caravans with tarps hung over the spaces between them. They walked along the edge of the old airport with weeds growing up through cracks in the asphalt like magic green reclaiming its scene. They walked down a road that had no sidewalk, just a ragged gravel edge, and below the road ran a creek in a gully of reeds.

They eventually found a spot not too far away from an intersection where a light would stop the cars. This time, their shelter was an abandoned bus in an empty dirt lot next to an access road. There were no stores or businesses or homes nearby, and only occasional cars seemed to pass. Michelle, her eyes barely open and her coat pulled tight around her, collapsed in a seat on the bus. T sat at the driver's seat and grinned and pushed the pedals and turned the wheel. Arl stood beside Michelle and placed the back of his hand gently against her forehead. You feeling alright? he said. But she didn't respond. He pushed the hair back from her face and stroked the top of her head.

Hey, looks like Jones has found us! T said up front. And lo but there he was, Jones coming across the lot and listing like a galleon, one arm wrapped around the blanket he slept in rolled up like a cannon muzzle. He saw them and waved his free arm. And bearing a bright smile, his face a red glow of relief for finding them, he climbed onto the bus and dropped his carpet and sighed like a steam train coming into the station.

Why, what have we here? he said, standing beside T, one hand on his heart, the other on T's shoulder. He looked back down the center aisle at Michelle propped up in a seat and Arl standing next to her and said, It looks like you've found us a fine vessel, captain!

It'll do for now, Arl said.

And is that a stove it would appear? There in the back? A nice addition! Do you see? We'll have fire and warmth and hot food! Arl, you've outdone yourself this time! Like a hound after a hare!

T looked back. Oh yeah, he said. Look at that.

Ahhh, Michelle, and how do you fare? Jones wobbled on his feet but squinted at her with concern.

No need to worry about me, she said. I'm not the one to worry about. And she smiled.

My solicitation is strictly universal.

I have no idea what that means, she said.

Where've you been? T asked.

I was lost in the mire. I was beyond the pale. I thought I'd arrive in far Arden, had it squarely in my sights, you see, but in my haze I hit a dead end. How many of us have come up against the hand of fate? Black oiled gears interlocking as backwards turns the luminous wheel? I could have stepped fearlessly through traffic. And what cosmic veronicas did I perform that miraculously maneuvered me away from the cool abyss? I danced on the edge of the cliff! Our previous abode is obliterated, by the way. But I was able to retrieve a few of our sustainables. And he pulled at one end of the carpet, out of which rattled utensils and cups and clothes and Michelle's blanket which he picked up by a corner and carried over to her, laying it across her lap. She smiled again.

Just when I think you should have been left behind, she said.

We only go on, Jones said.

You always seem to come up with something, T said.

God smiles even on the lowest of us. Not that we *are* low. No no no. Our bounty is immeasurable.

Well, bountiful as we may be, Arl said, we still have practical concerns.

I suppose it's my turn, Jones said.

Probably, Arl said, but I'll go. I'm feeling lucky, as you might say.

Strike while the iron is hot! Jones said.

You should let Jones go, Michelle said.

I want to, Arl said, and he stepped around Jones after giving him a slap on the shoulder and saying so that only Jones could hear, Good job getting the stuff. We'll be better now.

Only glad that I could contribute. I do understand that I have been…a bit cosmically absent of late.

Any port in a storm, Arl said, and looked down at the things scattered from the carpet.

Ah, he said and took the cardboard sign and folded it under his arm and went down the steps.

Good luck, buddy, T said.

Arl turned and looked up at T. Don't leave her alone, he said.

I won't, hey.

Get her to eat if you can. Anything, ok? I think there's another can of soup left.

T gave him a little salute and pulled the bus doors closed.

Arl crossed the lot, scanning for a trapdoor. There was bound to be one somewhere. The air was crackling with dry lightning coming through a cut in clouds bunched up like boxing gloves and rolling in from the east with just a flicker, the kind of thing that makes people gather frankincense and myrrh. A trapdoor might appear anywhere, in the ground, in an oak tree, sometimes high in the middle of the air. Some might stare at it in disbelief or think they've gone off their rocker or that it's a trick or nothing but a brain glitch. But not Arl. He's taken the leap more than once. Crawled through the onion with no guarantee of coming out at all and no idea what that other side might be. He might materialize in a wall, be stuck there till doomsday wailing in the amen corner. That's happened, batting away at cobwebs but unable to pull off the bright nightgown. And for a split moment he caught a glimpse of that white field you cross and cross till a trapdoor reveals itself. He's got to be ready to leap! It's not a time for hemming and hawing or slogging through the underground with its glass tubes shooting holes through to the surface, light coming down like dust falling on the brow of a scholar hunkered over a book. Let it all sink it, ladders going up and down through the sepia dream swirl and people crisscrossing like shoppers looking for a bargain on apocalypse. The gut-clench, Ooooooh, I hope I made the right decision! Even if he comes out in a bright-lit cafeteria shoveling mashed potatoes into his mouth or in a plush hotel bar with a lounge singer and grand piano gleaming like a coffin lid with characters standing around saying Elegant Oh we must summer there or deep in a gold vein under a miner's cap thin beam of light and that smell of oil and ringing in the ears or in that dead horse at the end of the street with shop windows lit by gas jets and sewer mains rattling and dripping while people with stork masks and skin peeling like seaweed from the pox of a bad age build their floral rock heaps with rats underfoot and pathways over rubble and those rays coming down and people above reaching down like they want to rescue their own reflections from the river. That's the gist of it. Standing on the corner of First and Despair, that worker going away at the two-by-fours in mad-dash movements swinging a buzz saw up and down, and he just knows, just knows, and then sure enough he hits his thigh and cuts it open so fast not even blood knows it can go anywhere, flesh like lunch meat, sirens already wailing before he makes it to the wharfs. Tent camps. Caravans. Drumfires. Random fights, who knows the reason, and someone taking off after a cheap shot. No one's going to chase him down. Walking through walls like they were nothing but afterthoughts. Walking through corridors like throats of disease. Coming out in drip water canyons, the far city towers in sluggish sunset fogbanks. Slogging through creek bottoms, trying to listen to his own head to hear what language this is, awake and aware, a portal-leaping, dimension-tripping traveler, not just a blind slug in a bag of bones wriggling in the dark and throwing punches at nothing like a gurgling sideshow left-over. Crack the head, brain leaking its inky yolk, sungazing so hard the eyes become world-absorbing flowers of fire. And even the blind feeling forward, house in the dark, ghosts vying for space, clingers, hangers-on mad as wet cats, spitting mad if you move one item out of place that's not really there anyway, plopping down in a train car opposite a man with a gold tooth sucking on a cigar and squinting and giving you the eye and saying right through the skull with no sound as such, What're you lookin at, boy? The ones drifting through with their twilight agendas and the smell of end of the world cabins, jugglers, magicians, drifters sticking their faces into people's heads, black blobs popping up in an exhale or a streetlamp right at that moment he takes the perfect picture. The bus that's always there and never goes anywhere, full of people wondering, why aren't we moving? Seen it all. Seen the hammering man and the lusty lady in stand-off, the beast-squid rising from the deep while he sings home hey home hey home, only to rise drained and gray and crossing the empty arcade as papers float down the empty Sunday street wrapping fast around his legs like leeches while he yanks them off while more and more slap against his arms and legs and chest and face, thickening up so he can't even breathe, so he writhes and twists and kicks thin air and someone sees him struggling and runs to help and pulls those papers away, but he's not there.

Arl stood for a moment, deciding which way to go. Not one vehicle appeared, and he wondered if he made a bad decision choosing this spot for them. He tapped the ground with his foot. Then a truck loaded with gravel came rumbling by and bits of gravel grit came flying off its haul and hit him as it passed. Then another car came and went. The sky was a low ceiling of throat-singers. Wind rose up as if bringing a new storm or dragging the old one with it. A stoplight in the intersection up ahead began to sway. That seemed like a good omen. He went and stood beneath it by the side of the road.

THE INVISIBLE HAND AND THE LEXICON OF THE ECONOMIC PARADIGM

Random walk

Impossible to predict the next step. EfficientMarketTheory says that the prices of many financial assets, such as shares, follow a random walk. In other words, there is no way of knowing whether the next change in the price will be up or down, or by how much it will rise or fall. The reason is that in an efficient market, all the information that would allow an investor to predict the next price move is already reflected in the current price. This belief has led some economists to argue that investors cannot consistently outperform the market. But some economists argue that asset prices are predictable (they follow a non-random walk) and that markets are not efficient.

Asymmetric shock

When something unexpected happens that affects one economy (or part of an economy) more than the rest. This can create big problems for policymakers if they are trying to set a macroeconomic policy that works for both the area affected by the shock and the unaffected area. For instance, some economic areas may be oil exporters and thus highly dependent on the price of oil, but other areas are not. If the oil price plunges, the oil-dependent area would benefit from policies designed to boost demand that might be unsuited to the needs of the rest of the economy. This may be a constant problem for those responsible for setting the interest rate for the euro given the big differences-

-and different potential exposures to shocks--among the economies within the eurozone.

Bounded rationality

A theory of human decision making that assumes that people behave rationally, but only within the limits of the information available to them. Because their information may be inadequate (bounded) they make take decisions that appear to be irrational according to traditional theories about homo economicus (economic man). (See also behavioural economics.)

Paris Club

The name given to the arrangements through which countries reschedule their official debt; that is, money borrowed from other governments rather than banks or private firms. The club is based on Avenue Kléber in Paris. Its members are the 19 founders of the Organisation of Economic Co-Operation and Development (OECD)as well as Russia. Other institutions such as the World Bank attend in an informal role. Rescheduling requires the consensus agreement of members and must not favour one creditor nation over another. Private debt rescheduling takes place through the London Club.

Animal spirits

The colourful name that economist John Maynard Keynes gave to one of the essential ingredients of economic prosperity: confidence. According to Keynes, animal spirits are a particular sort of confidence, "naive optimism". He meant this in the sense that, for entrepreneurs in particular, "the thought of ultimate loss which often overtakes pioneers, as experience undoubtedly tells us and them, is put aside as a healthy man puts aside the expectation of death". Where these animal spirits come from is something of a mystery. Certainly, attempts by politicians and others to talk up confidence by making optimistic noises about economic prospects have rarely done much good.

Mean reversion

The tendency for subsequent observations of a random variable to be closer to its mean than the current observation. For example, if the current number is seven, the average is five, and there is mean reversion, then the next observation is more likely to be six than eight.

Safe harbour

Protection from the rough seas of regulation. Laws and regulations often include a safe harbour clause that sets out the circumstances in which otherwise regulated firms or individuals can do something without regulatory oversight or interference.

Hawala

An ancient system of moving money based on trust. It predates western bank practices. Although it is now more associated with the Middle East, a version of hawala existed in China in the second half of the Tang dynasty (618-907), known as fei qian, or flying money. In hawala, no money moves physically between locations; nowadays it is transferred by means of a telephone call or fax between dealers in different countries. No legal contracts are involved, and recipients are given only a code number or simple token, such as a low-value banknote torn in half, to prove that money is due. Over time, transactions in opposite directions cancel each other out, so physical movement is minimised. Trust is the only capital that the dealers have. With it, the users of hawala have a worldwide money-transmission service that is cheap, fast and free of bureaucracy.

From a government's point of view, however, informal money networks are threatening, since they lie outside official channels that are regulated and taxed. They fear they are used by criminals, including terrorists. Although this is probably true, by far the main users of hawala networks are overseas workers, who do not trust official money transfer methods or cannot afford them, remitting earnings to their families.

Prisoners' dilemma

A favourite example in game theory, which shows why co-operation is difficult to achieve even when it is mutually beneficial. Two prisoners have been arrested for the same offence and are held in different cells. Each has two options: confess, or say nothing. There are three possible outcomes. One could confess and agree to testify against the other as a state witness, receiving a light sentence while his fellow prisoner receives a heavy sentence. They can both say nothing and may be lucky and get light sentences or even be let off, owing to lack of firm evidence. Or they may both confess and probably get lighter individual sentences than one would have received had he said nothing and the other had testified against him. The second outcome would be the best for both prisoners. However, the risk that the other might confess and turn state witness is likely to encourage both to confess, landing both with sentences that they might have avoided had they been able to co-operate in remaining silent. In an oligopoly, firms often behave like these prisoners, not setting prices as high as they could do if they only trusted the other firms not to undercut them. As a result, they are worse off.

Zero-sum game
When the gains made by winners in an economic transaction equal the losses suffered by the losers. It is identified as a special case in game theory. Most economic transactions are in some sense positive-sum games. But in popular discussion of economic issues, there are often examples of a mistaken zero-sum mentality, such as "profit comes at the expense of wages", "higher productivity means fewer jobs", and "imports mean fewer jobs here".

(from: https://www.economist.com/economics-a-to-z)

ABOUT THE AUTHOR

Douglas Cole has published eight poetry collections, including *The Cabin at the End of the World*, winner of the Best Book Award in Urban Poetry and the International Impact Book Award. His novel, *The White Field*, won the American Fiction Award, and his screenplay of *The White Field* won Best Unproduced Screenplay award in the Elegant Film Festival. His work has appeared in journals such as *Beloit Poetry, Fiction International, Valpariaso, The Gallway Review* and *Two Hawks Quarterly*. He also contributes a column called "Trading Fours" to the magazine, *Jerry Jazz Musician*. He received the Leslie Hunt Memorial prize in poetry, the Best of Poetry Award from Clapboard House, First Prize in the "Picture Worth 500 Words" from *Tattoo Highway*, and the Editors' Choice Award in fiction by *RiverSedge*. He has been nominated Eight times for a Pushcart and Nine times for Best of the Net. His website is https://douglast-cole.com.

ABOUT THE PRESS

Sea Crow Press is committed to amplifying voices that might otherwise go unheard. In a rapidly changing world, we believe the small press plays an essential part in contemporary arts as a community forum, a cultural reservoir, and an agent of change. We are international with a focus on our New England roots. We publish creative nonfiction, literary fiction, and poetry. Our books celebrate our connection to each other and to the natural world with a focus on positive change and great storytelling. We follow a traditional publishing model to create carefully selected and edited books. In turbulent times, we focus on sharing works of beauty that chart a positive course for the future.

We welcome emerging writers, experienced authors, and all readers.